PENGUIN BOOKS

Good Morning, Midnight

Jean Rhys was born in Dominica in 1890, the daughter of a Welsh doctor and a white Creole mother. When she was sixteen she came to England, where, after her father died, she drifted into a series of demimonde jobs – chorus girl, mannequin, artist's model.

She began to write when the first of her three marriages broke up. She was in her thirties by then and living in Paris, where she was encouraged by Ford Madox Ford (who also discovered D. H. Lawrence). Ford wrote an enthusiastic introduction to her first book in 1927, a collection of stories called *The Left Bank.* This was followed by *Quartet* (originally *Postures*, 1928), *After Leaving Mr Mackenzie* (1930), *Voyage in the Dark* (1934) and *Good Morning, Midnight* (1939). None was particularly successful, no doubt because all were decades ahead of their time in theme and tone, dealing as they did with women as underdogs, exploited for, and exploiting, their sexuality. With the outbreak of war and subsequent failure of *Good Morning, Midnight*, the books went out of print, and Jean Rhys dropped completely out of sight. It was generally thought that she was dead. Nearly twenty years later she was rediscovered, largely due to the enthusiasm of the writer Francis Wyndham. She was living reclusively in Cornwall, and during those years had accumulated the stories collected in *Tigers are Better-Looking.* In 1966 she made a sensational reappearance with *Wide Sargasso Sea,* which won the Royal Society of Literature Award and the W. H. Smith Award for that year. Her only comment on her sudden great success was 'It has come too late'. Her final collection of stories, *Sleep It Off Lady*, appeared in 1976, and *Smile Please*, her unfinished autobiography, was published posthumously in 1979. She was made a Fellow of the Royal Society of Literature in 1966 and a CBE in 1978.

Jean Rhys, described by A. Alvarez as 'one of the finest British writers of this century', died in 1979.

A. L. Kennedy is the author of three collections of stories and three novels, including the highly acclaimed *Everything You Need* (1999); and two non-fiction works. Her books have won a number of awards, including the Somerset Maugham Award, the Saltire First d the Mail on Sunday/John Llewellyn Rhys Prize. She has also written a number of plays and scripts for television and film, including the screenplay for the feature film *Stella Does Tricks* (1997).

JEAN RHYS

Good Morning, Midnight

With an Introduction by A. L. Kennedy

PENGUIN BOOKS

PENGUIN BOOKS

Published by the Penguin Group
Penguin Books Ltd, 27 Wrights Lane, London W8 5TZ, England
Penguin Putnam Inc., 375 Hudson Street, New York, New York 10014, USA
Penguin Books Australia Ltd, Ringwood, Victoria, Australia
Penguin Books Canada Ltd, 10 Alcorn Avenue, Toronto, Ontario, Canada M4V 3B2
Penguin Books India (P) Ltd, 11, Community Centre, Panchsheel Park, New Delhi – 110 017, India
Penguin Books (NZ) Ltd, Private Bag 102902, NSMC, Auckland, New Zealand
Penguin Books (South Africa) (Pty) Ltd, 5 Watkins Street, Denver Ext 4, Johannesburg 2094, South Africa

Penguin Books Ltd, Registered Offices: Harmondsworth, Middlesex, England

First published by Constable 1939
This edition published by André Deutsch 1967
Published in Penguin Books 1969
Reprinted 1975, 1978, 1980, 1981, 1984, 1987
Reprinted with a new Introduction in Penguin Classics 2000
2

Printed and bound in Great Britain by Clays Ltd, St Ives plc
Set in Linotype Baskerville

Introduction

The world of Jean Rhys's fiction is both strange and unnervingly familiar. Anyone who has ever been lonely, uncertain, afraid will find something of themselves here; something of the insidious, banal horror of a simply unhappy life. Anyone who has ever been surprised by a moment of intensity, by the peculiar beauties of everyday life will rediscover the almost physical impact of such encounters in Rhys's work. Splintered and melancholic, even surreal, it is still rarely anything less than powerful. Human emotions are leant a dreadful articulacy as they slither towards the edge of reasonable endurance via periods of boredom and desperation, fragile optimism and pure slapstick. Grief is saved from self-indulgence by a vitriolic humour and an uncanny, even disturbing, gift for observation.

Rhys has a voracious – and, for her time, quite literally indecent – appetite for detail: the odour of shabby rooms, the qualities of sunlight, the imperfections of cheap cloth, the implications of a smile, the demands and pains of bodies which both isolate and bewilder their inhabitants. Vivid fragments of sensory information swoop and lunge at the reader, establishing the rhythms of a bad drinking bout: one moment all docile clarity, the next a crush of sickened self-awareness, a lurch into the past, or a dreamscape, or a helpless re-examination of realities too dull and terrible to seem anything other than the products of a sick imagination.

Uniting each display of dark energy, irony and observation is Rhys's voice, the one constant in each treacherous landscape of uncertainty and flux. Known for her constant, almost obsessive, reworking of passages, Rhys had an admirable grip on the musicality of her prose, capitalizing on the ability of rhythm and melody to take the reader beyond what their social conditioning and their psychological experience might find entirely comfortable or likely. This sense of over-arching rhythm can bind together jumps in time and viewpoint, sections of impressionistic interior monologue, social comedy and lament, marking them as the unmistakable fruits of one mind, one desire to communicate.

Her style is plain, dry and full of the understatement readers might find typical of the English mindset Rhys so frequently derides. When Sophia Jansen, the protagonist of *Good Morning, Midnight,* announces that 'Life is curious when it is reduced to its essentials.' Readers already know enough to understand that for 'curious' we might just as well read 'hellish', 'unendurable' or 'fascinating' as Jansen ricochets between morbid delight and misery in her dissection of her self, its eccentricities and woes. The reduction Rhys refers to so blandly has already corroded Jansen's relationship with both her own body and her mind and has left her with little more than gallows humour, a taste for absinthe and a drive towards self-destruction. Like Melville's Ahab who declares 'All visible objects . . . are but as pasteboard masks', she no longer has faith, even in reality, but we first meet her where Ahab ends: alone and drowning. The fact that her 'deep, dark river' is entirely metaphorical seems less than a mercy.

Although *Good Morning, Midnight* is Sophia Jansen's first outing, Rhys has, in fact, approached versions of this character before. In her three preceding books the author appears to test virtually the same turn-of-the-century woman against three marginal existences, patched together out of disreputable jobs, poisonous liaisons and sexual alienation, all to the accompaniment of missed meals and the increasingly welcome release of alcohol. With each novel the protagonist is slightly older and slightly reworked, the details and depth of her past adjusted, the narrative viewpoint shifted, perhaps in search of an ideal.

In the first novel of the series, *Quartet*, young Marya Zelli is an English former chorus girl, trapped in poverty and a cynical, unwelcoming Paris when her ne'er-do-well husband is imprisoned for theft. She falls into an unfulfilling, yet compelling *ménage à trois*, which leaves her virtually broken and apparently irreparably sullied. Next, *After Leaving Mr Mckenzie* finds Julia Martin in Paris and already entirely reliant upon the money given her by ex-lover, Mr Mckenzie. When this support is withdrawn, she seeks consolation and further funds in London, only to meet with failure and an eventual return to Paris, reduced to even bleaker dependence and bitterness. A miserable and judgmental London makes a further appearance in *Voyage in the Dark*, where Anna Morgan, a chorus girl, spends 1914 becoming a virtual and then an actual prostitute.

Raised in the West Indies, she is plagued by a constant lack of colour, flavour and, above all, warmth. Paranoid, self-loathing, apparently emotionally anaesthetized and yet deeply needy, Anna seems intent upon either shocking herself back into sensation or erasing what remains of her personality. She experiences a tenuous happiness as the mistress of a Mr Jeffries before the inevitable abandonment. The book ends with the abortion of her first child and the, by now dreadful, persistence of her life.

Good Morning, Midnight takes Sophia Jansen from London and a much-begrudged allowance from relatives and sets her back in the Paris she once knew well. A noticeably older woman than Rhys's preceding heroines, she is a former mannequin and has, since leaving that *métier*, botched a succession of unsatisfying jobs. We see her desert her last post, as a toweringly bored assistant in a dress shop. Having already come to '. . . the bright idea of drinking myself to death,' Jansen wanders the city, helpless to prevent it reminding her of her first, exciting, but painful marriage to Dutchman, Enno Jansen, and of their infant child's death. Almost beyond sexuality and haunted by her own ageing, she seems immune to the advances of artists, fellow drifters and a particularly determined gigolo, but is ultimately betrayed by her body's almost inexpressible need for comfort.

Rhys herself was brought up in the West Indies, had a legendary fondness for drink and had, of course, worked as a chorus girl, a mannequin and an artist's model, if not an artist. *Quartet* first appeared in 1928, a year after her first book, *The Left Bank*, a collection of short stories which included an enthusiastic, if proprietorial, introduction from editor Ford Maddox Ford, the man who had 'discovered' her in Paris. He was also the man whose mistress she had become within a painful Parisian *ménage à trois*. The novel's unremitting exploration of all the most grisly nooks and crannies of just such a nocturnal triangle underline Rhys's steadfastly merciless appropriation of autobiographical material. If it were not for the psychological depth she brings to her work, she might seem a voyeuse in her own life. Turning her back on fictions more distant from her actual experience, she chooses to make only inward journeys, wringing different truths from old facts, exposing her protagonists and her readers to an almost wounding kind of intimacy. Attacking key elements of her past, regardless of their sensitivity, she seems to seek their transformation, using the catalyst of a single, dominant and deeply exposed character. With Jansen and *Good Morning, Midnight* Rhys could be said to have finally reached her ideal rendition of her imagined stranger's – and, thereby, her own – life. This is the version she had been searching for in the course of four novels.

Jansen is both the most desperate and the strongest of Rhys's heroines to this date and emerges as a mature creation, even in comparison with Antoinette Cosway of the much later and better known *Wide Sargasso Sea*. We meet Jansen at a point somewhere a touch beyond the end of her tether. Her pain is remarkable, her self-obsession sometimes smothering and sometimes quite intentionally hilarious, but she also offers great discipline as a narrator. Rhys seems to relax as never before in her depiction of Jansen, creating a woman who, having decided to die, gains a strange dignity and the perfect distance from which to observe her own ruin. There is a resultant ease and a sense of organic cohesion as *Good Morning, Midnight* weaves characteristically – and at an astonishing pace – in and out of flashback, paranoid projection, breaks of farce and glimpses of tangibly wasted promise when, as Jansen puts it, she sees 'my beautiful life in front of me, opening out like a fan in my hand . . .' Jansen's quintessentially deadpan delivery is so firmly established by Rhys that the simple ellipsis into which the sentence dwindles audibly heralds a less than charming future. With Jansen, Rhys has the confidence to prove that less is more.

By making Jansen her fictional drinking partner, Rhys adds the missing element that makes complete sense of a turbulent, shattered narrative. The temporal and emotional shifts of vocational drinking are rendered perfectly here and seem to allow Rhys to have more fun with her creation, to delight in more teases and word plays and in the lighter-hearted transgressions of politesse which culminate in Jansen stepping calmly out of her fallen drawers in the middle of the street and folding them into her handbag. This is a woman past saving but not beyond humanity and even spasms of hope: someone whose company is pleasant, even when her story is not. Rhys endows her with genuinely compelling passion as she introduces herself and, in the process, cries out on behalf of any underdog.

> . . . I am an inefficient member of society, slow in the uptake, slightly damaged in the fray, there's no denying it. So you have the right to pay me four hundred francs a month, to lodge me in a small, dark room, to clothe me shabbily, to harass me with worry and monotony and unsatisfied longings till you get me to the point where I blush at a look, cry at a word.

It is in *Good Morning, Midnight* that Rhys most clearly joins the likes of Jim Thompson, Venedikt Yerofeev and Fred Exley in the specialized field of alcohol-induced social commentary. Like them, she found her considerable intelligence terribly and wonderfully powerless to resist dissolution in drink. Her protagonist, like theirs, rails against a world she has drunk herself out of, against the iniquities, petty distinctions and hypocrisies of normal life. Jansen despises normality, she wants the liquid that will take away her problems and give her, '. . . more of this feeling – fire and wings'. And yet the loathing isn't simple disgust: it's the rage of a spurned lover, of wounded pride, of massive self-loathing trying to balance itself by detesting all it meets. Jansen knows she can no longer make the grade in every day life, she has become irretrievably alien and isolated. A change of hair colour, a new dress, a new hotel room, a new name: nothing will quite work the magic that could bring her the comfort of feeling human within the mass of humanity. In a voice which is both bitter and longing to be contradicted she recites, 'Please, please, monsieur et madame, mister, missis and miss. I am trying so hard to be like you. I know I don't succeed but look how hard I try.' But, of course, there is no one to contradict her, she is speaking to herself.

Rhys, naturally, differs from the usual litany of chemical outsiders in being a woman and portraying women caught in a society largely intimical to them, even if they choose to conform to its every restriction. Jansen is not just a drunk, but a drunk woman, the lowest of the low. This, along with Rhys's stylistic experimentation and her choice of 'unsuitable' subject matter, helped to make her work, and perhaps this book most of all, ahead of its time – the literary euphemism for difficult to place, low-selling and initially quick to disappear. Today, these qualities give her writing a modern and still surprisingly penetrative, impact. *Good Morning, Midnight* combines a pervasive sense of broad social injustice, along with parallel sexual injustices and also compels us to face the particular, to show us a protagonist destroyed not only by her own fatal flaws, but by those of the society around her.

This is not to suggest that Rhys preaches, or even appears noticeably politicized – her work is far more subtle than that. She presents the unnecessary suffering and cruelty of the world, but offers no neat remedies. Our compassion for Jansen is rewarded only with the sight of another injury to her physical or mental well-being, or with the kind of dark comedy that has her pantomime the unwilling unborn, trying to wriggle out of their date with earthly existence. 'Oh, not me, please, not me. Well then, you, Y, you go along and be born – somebody's got to be.'

And, yet, within Jansen there are the unmistakable traces of positive alternatives, potential and the unmistakable outline of something heroic. Because Rhys, in *Good Morning, Midnight* has genuinely managed to overturn, what is even now, still the expected balance, both of society and the novel. Jansen, a woman, is the one fully formed character; the one mind clearly displaying its ability to be equal to any other. The men who ghost in and out of the narrative, even when they have a violent impact on Jansen's life, have a certain lack of substance. One might argue that Rhys simply wasn't good at writing fully-realized men – that her one attempt in *Wide Sargasso Sea* was not entirely a success. But it could equally be suggested that Rhys had no interest in producing fully-realized men, that she intended to surround her women with men who are largely as shallow, weak, spiteful and vain as the stereotypical woman is supposed to be. From Jansen's perspective – and we always do see from Jansen's perspective – men are of peripheral importance. They wield a power they may not deserve, or be able to control, but they rarely have any genuine stature. Even the delights of their bodies seem to be a gift they don't understand and barely know how to bestow.

This is not to say that Rhys is entirely set against her opposite sex – she is simply and sharply aware of the kind of man self-destructive women are drawn to. Jansen, for example, meets with an impoverished artist who has little interest in her money, shares her (and Rhys's) loathing of London and seems to be a person of honour, if some eccentricity. After arranging a further meeting, Jansen, of course, makes sure she never sees him again. She wants, and acquires, men who will resemble her drug of choice, who will overwhelm her, rip her into a state of forgetfulness and then leave her behind, damaged and stripped of her dignity.

Of all the temptations and torments which afflict Jansen and Rhys's other creations, those which are the most terrible and the most finely worked all lie in her depictions of relationships. She maps out the clashes of interest that worm between lovers, the flurries of ego, the pettiness and tenderness, the ability of a loved one to call up simultaneous, and entirely conflicting, emotions. Her eloquence in the language of human sexual transactions is chilling, cynical and surprisingly moving. Partners are drawn together by the very qualities which will eventually lead them to hate and injure each other and themselves. There is no redemptive love here, as Englishwoman Jansen says, 'Love is a stern virtue in England.' It seems no less stern in Paris. Perhaps appropriately, her story ends with a potential lover's act of cruel kindness and another's sexual theft. We understand why Jansen tells us, 'People talk about the happy life, but that's the happy life when you don't care any longer if you live or die.' And, once again, we wish to contradict her, if only in our own, personal narratives.

Publisher's Note in the 1967 André Deutsch edition

Good Morning, Midnight was first published in 1939, by Constable. Its reappearance in this edition seems an appropriate occasion on which to recall that it was through this novel that we became able to publish Jean Rhys's complete works.

We had not been able to discover the whereabouts of Jean Rhys until, in 1957, an adaptation of *Good Morning, Midnight* was broadcast on the BBC's Third Programme. This adaptation was made and read by Miss Selma Vaz Dias. When we got in touch with Miss Vaz Dias to congratulate her on it – it was strikingly successful – we found that, having pursued the matter with great determination and devotion because of her admiration for the art of Jean Rhys, she had achieved what we had failed to achieve and could give us Miss Rhys's address. She also told us that Miss Rhys was beginning work on a new novel, *Wide Sargasso Sea*, which became the first of her books published by us (October 1966).

Now on the appearance of *Good Morning, Midnight* simultaneously with *Voyage in the Dark*, which marks the beginning of our republication of the earlier novels, we would like to thank Miss Vaz Dias for her part in the rediscovery of Jean Rhys.

Good morning, Midnight!
I'm coming home,
Day got tired of me –
How could I of him?

Sunshine was a sweet place,
I liked to stay –
But Morn didn't want me – now –
So good night, Day!

EMILY DICKINSON

Part One

'Quite like old times,' the room says. 'Yes? No?'

There are two beds, a big one for madame and a smaller one on the opposite side for monsieur. The wash-basin is shut off by a curtain. It is a large room, the smell of cheap hotels faint, almost imperceptible. The street outside is narrow, cobble-stoned, going sharply uphill and ending in a flight of steps. What they call an impasse.

I have been here five days. I have decided on a place to eat in at midday, a place to eat in at night, a place to have my drink in after dinner. I have arranged my little life.

The place to have my drink in after dinner. ... Wait, I must be careful about that. These things are very important

Last night, for instance. Last night was a catastrophe. ... The woman at the next table started talking to me – a dark, thin woman of about forty, very well made-up. She had the score of a song with her and she had been humming it under her breath, tapping the accompaniment with her fingers.

'I like that song.'

'Ah, yes, but it's a sad song. *Gloomy Sunday.*' She giggled. 'A little sad.'

She was waiting for her friend, she told me.

The friend arrived – an American. He stood me another brandy-and-soda and while I was drinking it I started to cry.

I said: 'It was something I remembered.'

The dark woman sat up very straight and threw her chest out.

'I understand,' she said, 'I understand. All the same. ... Sometimes I'm just as unhappy as you are. But that's not to say that I let everybody see it.'

Unable to stop crying, I went down into the lavabo. A familiar lavabo, and luckily empty. The old dame was outside near the telephone, talking to a girl.

I stayed there, staring at myself in the glass. What do I want to cry about? ... On the contrary, it's when I am quite sane like this, when I have had a couple of extra drinks and am quite sane, that I realize how lucky I am. Saved, rescued, fished-up, half-drowned, out of the deep, dark river, dry clothes, hair shampooed and set. Nobody would know I had ever been in it. Except, of course, that there always remains something. Yes, there always remains something. ... Never mind, here I am, sane and dry, with my place to hide in. What more do I want? ... I'm a bit of an automaton, but sane, surely – dry, cold and sane. Now I have forgotten about dark streets, dark rivers, the pain, the struggle and the drowning. ... Mind you, I'm not talking about the struggle when you are strong and a good swimmer and there are willing and eager friends on the bank waiting to pull you out at the first sign of distress. I mean the real thing. You jump in with no willing and eager friends around, and when you sink you sink to the accompaniment of loud laughter.

Lavabos. ... What about that monograph on lavabos – toilets – ladies? ... A London lavabo in black and white marble, fifteen women in a queue, each clutching her penny, not one bold spirit daring to dash out of her turn past the stern-faced attendant. That's what I call discipline. ... The lavabo in Florence and the very pretty, fantastically dressed girl who rushed in, hugged and kissed the old dame tenderly and fed her with cakes out of a paper bag. The dancer-daughter? ... That cosy little Paris lavabo, where the attendant peddled drugs – something to heal a wounded heart.

When I got upstairs the American and his friend had

gone. 'It was something I remembered,' I told the waiter, and he looked at me blankly, not even bothering to laugh at me. His face was unsurprised, blank.

That was last night.

I lie awake, thinking about it, and about the money Sidonie lent me and the way she said: 'I can't bear to see you like this.' Half-shutting her eyes and smiling the smile which means: 'She's getting to look old. She drinks.'

'We've known each other too long, Sasha,' she said, 'to stand on ceremony with each other.'

I had just come in from my little health-stroll round Mecklenburgh Square and along the Gray's Inn Road. I had looked at this, I had looked at that, I had looked at the people passing in the street and at a shop-window full of artificial limbs. I came in to somebody who said: 'I can't bear to see you looking like this.'

'Like what?' I said.

'I think you need a change. Why don't you go back to Paris for a bit? ... You could get yourself some new clothes – you certainly need them. ... I'll lend you the money,' she said. 'I'll be over there next week and I could find a room for you if you like.' Etcetera, etcetera.

I had not seen this woman for months and then she swooped down on me. ... Well, here I am. When you've been made very cold and very sane you've also been made very passive. (Why worry, why worry?)

I can't sleep. Rolling from side to side....

Was it in 1923 or 1924 that we lived round the corner, in the Rue Victor-Cousin, and Enno bought me that Cossack cap and the imitation astrakhan coat? It was then that I started calling myself Sasha. I thought it might change my luck if I changed my name. Did it bring me any luck, I wonder – calling myself Sasha?

Was it in 1926 or 1927?

I put the light on. The bottle of Evian on the bedtable, the tube of luminal, the two books, the clock ticking on the ledge, the red curtains....

I can see Sidonie carefully looking round for an hotel just like this one. She imagines that it's my atmosphere. God, it's an insult when you come to think about it! More dark rooms, more red curtains....

But one mustn't put everything on the same plane. That's her great phrase. And one mustn't put everybody on the same plane, either. Of course not. And this is my plane.... Quatrième à gauche, and mind you don't trip over the hole in the carpet. That's me.

There are some black specks on the wall. I stare at them, certain they are moving. Well, I ought to be able to ignore a few bugs by this time. 'Il ne faut pas mettre tout sur le même plan....'

I get up and look closely. Only splashes of dirt. It's not the time of year for bugs, anyway.

I take some more luminal, put the light out and sleep at once.

I am in the passage of a tube station in London. Many people are in front of me; many people are behind me. Everywhere there are placards printed in red letters: This Way to the Exhibition, This Way to the Exhibition. But I don't want the way to the exhibition – I want the way out. There are passages to the right and passages to the left, but no exit sign. Everywhere the fingers point and the placards read: This Way to the Exhibition.... I touch the shoulder of the man walking in front of me. I say: 'I want the way out.' But he points to the placards and his hand is made of steel. I walk along with my head bent, very ashamed, thinking: 'Just like me – always wanting to be different from other people.' The steel finger points along a long stone passage. This Way – This Way – This Way to the Exhibition....

Now a little man, bearded, with a snub nose, dressed in a long white night-shirt, is talking earnestly to me. 'I am your father,' he says. 'Remember that I am your father.' But blood is streaming from a wound in his forehead. 'Murder,' he shouts, 'murder, murder.' Helplessly I watch the blood streaming. At last my voice tears itself loose from my chest. I too shout: 'Murder, murder, help, help,' and the sound fills the room. I wake up and a man in the street outside is singing the waltz from *Les Saltimbanques*. 'C'est l'amour qui flotte dans l'air à ronde,' he sings.

I believe it's a fine day, but the light in this room is so bad that you can't be sure. Outside on the landing you can't see at all unless the electric light is on. It's a large landing, cluttered up from morning to night with brooms, pails, piles of dirty sheets and so forth – the wreckage of the spectacular floors below.

The man who has the room next to mine is parading about as usual in his white dressing-gown. Hanging around. He is like the ghost of the landing. I am always running into him.

He is as thin as a skeleton. He has a bird-like face and sunken, dark eyes with a peculiar expression, cringing, ingratiating, knowing. What's he want to look at me like that for? ... He is always wearing a dressing-gown – a blue one with black spots or the famous white one. I can't imagine him in street clothes.

'Bonjour.'

'Bonjour,' I mutter. I don't like this damned man....

When I get downstairs the patron tells me that he wants to see my passport. I haven't put the number of the passport on the fiche, he says.

This patron is exactly like one of the assistants who used to be in the pawnshop in the Rue de Rennes – the one who scowled at you and took your stuff away to be valued. A fish, lording it in his own particular tank, staring at the world outside with a glassy and unbelieving eye.

What's wrong with the fiche? I've filled it up all right, haven't I? Name So-and-so, nationality So-and-so. ... Nationality – that's what has puzzled him. I ought to have put nationality by marriage.

I tell him I will let him have the passport in the

afternoon and he gives my hat a gloomy, disapproving look. I don't blame him. It shouts 'Anglaise', my hat. And my dress extinguishes me. And then this damned old fur coat slung on top of everything else – the last idiocy, the last incongruity.

Never mind, I have some money now. I may be able to do something about it. Twelve o'clock on a fine autumn day, and nothing to worry about. Some money to spend and nothing to worry about.

But careful, careful! Don't get excited. You know what happens when you get excited and exalted, don't you? ... Yes. ... And then, you know how you collapse like a pricked balloon, don't you? Having no staying power. ... Yes, exactly. ... So, no excitement. This is going to be a quiet, sane fortnight. Not too much drinking, avoidance of certain cafés, of certain streets, of certain spots, and everything will go off beautifully.

The thing is to have a programme, not to leave anything to chance – no gaps. No trailing around aimlessly with cheap gramophone records starting up in your head, no 'Here this happened, here that happened'. Above all, no crying in public, no crying at all if you can help it.

Thinking all this, I pass the exact place for my after-dinner drink. It's a café on the Avenue de l'Observatoire, which always seems to be empty. I remember it like this before.

I'll go in and have a Pernod. Just one, just once, for luck. ... Here's to the Miracle, I'll say, to the Miracle. ...

A man who looks like an Arab comes in, accompanied by a melancholy girl wearing spectacles.

'Life is difficult,' the Arab says.

'Yes, life isn't easy,' the girl says.

Long pause.

'One needs a lot of courage, to live,' the Arab says.

'Ah, I believe you,' the girl says, shaking her head and clicking her tongue.

They finish their vermouth and go out and I sit alone

in a large, clean, empty room and watch myself in the long glass opposite, turning over the pages of an old number of *l'Illustration*, thinking that I haven't got a care in the world, except that tomorrow's Sunday – a difficult day anywhere. Sombre dimanche....

Planning it all out. Eating. A movie. Eating again. One drink. A long walk back to the hotel. Bed. Luminal. Sleep. Just sleep – no dreams.

At four o'clock next afternoon I am in a cinema on the Champs-Elysées, according to programme. Laughing heartily in the right places.

It's a very good show and I see it through twice. When I come out of the cinema it's night and the street lamps are lit. I'm glad of that. If you've got to walk around by yourself, it's easier when the lamps are lit.

Paris is looking very nice tonight. ... You are looking very nice tonight, my beautiful, my darling, and oh what a bitch you can be! But you didn't kill me after all, did you? And they couldn't kill me either....

Just about here we waited for a couple of hours to see Anatole France's funeral pass, because, Enno said, we mustn't let such a great literary figure disappear without paying him the tribute of a last salute.

There we were, chatting away affably, paying Anatole France the tribute of a last salute, and most of the people who passed in the procession were chatting away affably too, looking as if they were making dates for lunches and dinners, and we were all paying Anatole France the tribute of a last salute.

I walk along, remembering this, remembering that, trying to find a cheap place to eat – not so easy round here. The gramophone record is going strong in my head: 'Here this happened, here that happened....'

I used to work in a shop just off this street.

I can see myself coming out of the Métro station at the Rond-Point every morning at half-past eight, walking along the Avenue Marigny, turning to the left and then to the right, putting my coat and hat into the cloak-room, going along a passage and starting in with: 'Good morning, madame. Has madame a vendeuse?'

*

. . . It was a large white-and-gold room with a dark-polished floor. Imitation Louis Quinze chairs, painted screens, three or four elongated dolls, beautifully dressed, with charming and malicious oval faces.

Every time a customer arrived, the commissionaire touched a bell which rang just over my head. I would advance towards the three steps leading down to the street-door and stand there, smiling a small, discreet smile. I would say 'Good afternoon, madame. . . . Certainly, madame,' or 'Good afternoon, madame. Mademoiselle Mercédès has had your telephone message and everything is ready,' or 'Certainly, madame. . . . Has madame a vendeuse?'

Then I would conduct the customer to the floor above, where the real activities of the shop were carried on, and call for Mademoiselle Mercédès or Mademoiselle Henriette or Madame Perron, as the case might be. If I forgot a face or allotted a new customer to a saleswoman out of her turn, there was a row.

There was no lift in this shop. That's why I was there. It was one of those dress-houses still with a certain prestige – anyhow among the French – but its customers were getting fewer and fewer.

I had had the job for three weeks. It was dreary. You couldn't read; they didn't like it. I would feel as if I were drugged, sitting there, watching those damned dolls, thinking what a success they would have made of their lives if they had been women. Satin skin, silk hair, velvet eyes, sawdust heart – all complete. I used to envy the commissionaire, because at least he could watch the people passing in the street. On the other hand, he had to stand up all the time. Yes, perhaps I had rather be myself than the commissionaire.

There was always a very strong smell of scent. I would pretend that I could recognize the various scents. Today it's L'Heure Bleue; yesterday it was Nuits de Chine. ... The place also smelt of the polish on the floor, the old furniture, the dolls' clothes.

The shop had a branch in London, and the boss of the London branch had bought up the whole show. Every three months or so he came over to the French place and it was rumoured that he was due to arrive on a certain day. What's he like? Oh, he's the real English type. Very nice, very, very chic, the real English type, le businessman. ... I thought: 'Oh, my God, I know what these people mean when they say the real English type.'

... He arrives. Bowler-hat, majestic trousers, oh-my-God expression, ha-ha eyes – I know him at once. He comes up the steps with Salvatini behind him, looking very worried. (Salvatini is the boss of our shop.) Don't let him notice me, don't let him look at me. Isn't there something you can do so that nobody looks at you or sees you? Of course, you must make your mind vacant, neutral, then your face also becomes vacant, neutral – you are invisible.

No use. He comes up to my table.

'Good morning, good morning, Miss –'

'Mrs Jansen,' Salvatini says.

Shall I stand up or not stand up? Stand up, of course. I stand up.

'Good morning.'

I smile at him.

'And how many languages do you speak?'

He seems quite pleased. He smiles back at me. Affable, that's the word. I suppose that's why I think it's a joke.

'One,' I say, and go on smiling.

Now, what's happened? ... Oh, of course. ...

'I understand French quite well.'

He fidgets with the buttons on his coat.

'I was told that the receptionist spoke French and German fluently,' he says to Salvatini.

'She speaks French,' Salvatini says. 'Assez bien, assez bien.'

Mr Blank looks at me with lifted eyebrows.

'Sometimes,' I say idiotically.

Of course, sometimes, when I am a bit drunk and am talking to somebody I like and know, I speak French very fluently indeed. At other times I just speak it. And as to that, my dear sir, you've got everything all wrong. I'm here because I have a friend who knows Mr Salvatini's mistress, and Mr Salvatini's mistress spoke to Mr Salvatini about me, and the day that he saw me I wasn't looking too bad and he was in a good mood. Nothing at all to do with fluent French and German, dear sir, nothing at all. I'm here because I'm here because I'm here. And just to prove to you that I speak French, I'll sing you a little song about it: 'Si vous saviez, si vous saviez, si vous saviez comment ça se fait.'

For God's sake, I think, pull yourself together.

I say: 'I speak French fairly well. I've been living in Paris for eight years.'

No, he's suspicious now. Questions short and sharp.

'How long have you been working here?'

'About three weeks.'

'What was your last job?'

'I worked at the Maison Chose in the Place Vendôme.'

'Oh, really, you worked for Chose, did you? You worked for Chose.' His voice is more respectful. 'Were you receptionist there?'

'No,' I say. 'I worked as a mannequin.'

'You worked as a mannequin?' Down and up his eyes go, up and down. 'How long ago was this?' he says.

How long ago was it? Now, everything is a blank in my head – years, days, hours, everything is a blank in my head. How long ago was it? I don't know.

'Four, nearly five, years ago.'

'How long did you stay there?'

'About three months,' I say.

He seems to be waiting for further information.

'And then I left,' I say in a high voice. (Decidedly this is one of my good days. This is one of the days when I say everything right.)

'Oh, you left?'

'Yes, I left.'

Yes, my dear sir, I left. I got bored and I walked out on them. But that was four, nearly five, years ago and a lot can happen in five years. I haven't the slightest intention of walking out on you, I can assure you of that. And I hope you haven't the slightest intention of – And just the thought that you may have the slightest intention of – makes my hands go cold and my heart beat.

'Have you worked anywhere else since then?'

'Well, no. No, I haven't.'

'I see,' he says. He waves backwards and forwards like a tall tree that is going to fall on me. Then he makes a sound like 'Hah', and goes off into a room at the back, followed by Salvatini.

Well, this has gone badly, there's no disguising it. It has gone as badly as possible. It couldn't have gone worse. But it's over. Now he'll never notice me again; he'll forget about me.

An old Englishwoman and her daughter come into the shop. I escort them upstairs and then fidget about arranging the showcases at the back of the room. In an hour or so they come down again. They walk up to the showcases, the old lady eager, the daughter very reluctant.

'Can you show me some of these pretty things?' the old lady says. 'I want something to wear in my hair in the evening.'

She takes off her hat and she is perfectly bald on top – a white, bald skull with a fringe of grey hair. The daughter stays in the background. She is past shame, detached, grim.

'Come along, mother, do let's go. Don't be silly, mother. You won't find anything here.'

There is a long glass between the two windows. The old lady complacently tries things on her bald head.

The daughter's eyes meet mine in the mirror. Damned old hag, isn't she funny? ... I stare back at her coldly.

I will say for the old lady that she doesn't care a damn about all this. She points to various things and says: 'Show me that – show me that.' A sturdy old lady with gay, bold eyes.

She tried on a hair-band, a Spanish comb, a flower. A green feather waves over her bald head. She is calm and completely unconcerned. She was like a Roman emperor in that last thing she tried on.

'Mother, please come away. Do let's go.'

The old lady doesn't take the slightest notice, and she has everything out of both of the cases before she goes. Then: 'Well,' she says, 'I'm very sorry. I'm so sorry to have given you so much trouble.'

'It's no trouble at all, madame.'

As they go towards the door the daughter bursts out. A loud, fierce hiss: 'Well, you made a perfect fool of yourself, as usual. You've had everybody in the shop sniggering. If you want to do this again, you'll have to do it by yourself. I refuse, I refuse.'

The old lady does not answer. I can see her face reflected in a mirror, her eyes still undaunted but something about her mouth and chin collapsing. ... Oh, but why not buy her a wig, several decent dresses, as much champagne as she can drink, all the things she likes to eat and oughtn't to, a gigolo if she wants one? One last flare-up, and she'll be dead in six months at the outside. That's all you're waiting for, isn't it? But no, you must have the slow death, the bloodless killing that leaves no stain on your conscience....

I put the ornaments back in the cases slowly, carefully, just as they were.

That brings me up to déjeuner. I go upstairs. One long table here, the mannequins and saleswomen all mixed up.

There is, of course, an English mannequin. 'Kind, kind and gentle is she' – and that's another damned lie. But she is very beautiful – 'belle comme une fleur de verre'. And the other one, the little French one whom I like so much, she is 'Belle comme une fleur de terre. . . .'

I still can't get over the meal at this place. I have been living for some time on bread and coffee, and it blows my stomach out every time. Hors d'œuvres, plat du jour, vegetables, dessert. Coffee and a quarter of wine are extra, but so little extra that everybody has them.

Nobody talks about the English manager – a wary silence.

I go downstairs, feeling dazed and happy. Gradually the happiness goes; I am just dazed.

Salvatini puts his head out of the door behind me and says: 'Mr Blank wants to see you.'

I at once make up my mind that he wants to find out if I can speak German. All the little German I know flies out of my head. Jesus, Help me! Ja, ja, nein, nein, was kostet es, Wien ist eine sehr schöne Stadt, Buda-Pest auch ist sehr schön, ist schön, mein Herr, ich habe meinen Blumen vergessen, aus meinen grossen Schmerzen, homo homini lupus, aus meinen grossen Schmerzen mach ich die kleinen Lieder, homo homini lupus (I've got that one, anyway), aus meinen grossen Schmerzen homo homini doh ré mi fah soh la ti doh. . . .

He is sitting at the desk, writing a letter. I stand there. He is sure to notice how shabby my shoes are.

Salvatini looks up, gives me a furtive smile and then looks away again.

Come on, stand straight, keep your head up, smile. . . . No, don't smile. If you smile, he'll think you're trying to get off with him. I know his type. He won't give me the benefit of a shadow of a doubt. Don't smile then, but look eager, alert, attentive.... Run out of the door and get away.... You fool, stand straight, look eager, alert, attentive.... No, look here, he's doing this on purpose.... Of course he isn't doing it on purpose. He's just writing a letter.... He is, he is. He's doing it on purpose. I know it, I feel it. I've been standing here for five minutes. This is impossible.

'Did you wish to see me, Mr Blank?'

He looks up and says sharply: 'Yes, yes, what is it? What do you want? Wait a minute, wait a minute.'

At once I know. He doesn't want me to talk German, he's going to give me the sack. All right then, hurry up, get it over....

Nothing. I just stand there. Now panic has come on me. My hands are shaking, my heart is thumping, my hands are cold. Fly, fly, run from these atrocious voices, these abominable eyes....

He finishes his letter, writes a line or two on another piece of paper and puts it into an envelope.

'Will you please take this to the kise?'

Take this to the kise.... I look at Salvatini. He smiles encouragingly.

Mr Blank rattles out: 'Be as quick as you can, Mrs – er – please. Thank you very much.'

I turn and walk blindly through a door. It is a lavatory. They look sarcastic as they watch me going out by the right door.

I walk a little way along the passage, then stand with my back against the wall.

This is a very old house – two old houses. The first floor, the shop proper, is modernized. The showrooms, the fitting-rooms, the mannequins' room.... But on the ground floor are the workrooms and offices and dozens of small rooms, passages that don't lead anywhere, steps going up and steps going down.

Kise – kise.... It doesn't mean a thing to me. He's got me into such a state that I can't imagine what it can mean.

Now, no panic. This envelope must have a name on it. ... Monsieur L. Grousset.

Somewhere in this building is a Monsieur L. Grousset. I have got to take this letter to him. Easy. Somebody will tell me where his room is. Grousset, Grousset....

I turn to the right, walk along another passage, down a flight of stairs. The workrooms. ... No, I can't ask here. All the girls will stare at me. I shall seem such a fool.

I try another passage. It ends in a lavatory. The number of lavatories in this place, c'est inoui. ... I turn the corner, find myself back in the original passage and collide with a strange young man. He gives me a nasty look.

'Could you tell me, please, where I can find Monsieur Grousset?'

'Connais pas,' the young man says.

After this it becomes a nightmare. I walk up stairs, past doors, along passages – all different, all exactly alike. There is something very urgent that I must do. But I don't meet a soul and all the doors are shut.

This can't go on. Shall I throw the damned thing away and forget all about it?

'What you must do is this,' I tell myself: 'You must go back and say – quite calmly – "I'm very sorry, but I didn't understand where you wanted me to take this note."'

I knock. He calls out: 'Come in.' I go in.

He takes the note from my hand. He looks at me as if I were a dog which had presented him with a very, very old bone. (Say something, say something....)

'I couldn't find him.'

'But how do you mean you couldn't find him? He must be there.'

'I'm very sorry. I didn't know where to find him.'

'You don't know where to find the cashier – the counting-house?'

'La caisse,' Salvatini says – helpfully, but too late.

But if I tell him that it was the way he pronounced it

that confused me, it will seem rude. Better not say anything. ...

'Well, don't you know?'

'Yes, I do. Oh yes, I do know.'

That is to say, I knew this morning where the cashier's office is. It isn't so far from the place where we put our hats and coats. But I don't know a damned thing now. ... Run, run away from their eyes, run from their voices, run. ...

We stare at each other. I breathe in deeply and breathe out again.

'Extraordinary,' he says, very slowly, 'quite extraordinary. God knows I'm used to fools, but this complete imbecility. ... This woman is the biggest fool I've ever met in my life. She seems to be half-witted. She's hopeless. ... Well, isn't she?' he says to Salvatini.

Salvatini makes a rolling movement of his head, shoulders and eyes, which means; 'I quite agree with you. Deplorable, deplorable.' Also: 'She's not so bad as you think.' Also: 'Oh, my God, what's all this about? What a day, what a day! When will it be over?' Anything you like, Salvatini's shrug means.

Not to cry in front of this man. Tout, mais pas ça. Say something. ... No, don't say anything. Just walk out of the room.

'No, wait a minute,' he says. 'You'd better take that note along. You do know who to take it to now, don't you? The cashier.'

'Yes.'

He stares at me. Something else has come into his eyes. He knows how I am feeling – yes, he knows.

'Just a hopeless, helpless little fool, aren't you?' he says. Jovial? Bantering? On the surface, yes. Underneath? No, I don't think so.

'Well, aren't you?'

'Yes, yes, yes, yes. Oh, yes.'

I burst into tears. I haven't even got a handkerchief.

'Dear me,' Mr Blank says.

'Allons, allons,' Salvatini says. 'Voyons. . . .'

I rush away from them into a fitting-room. It is hardly ever used. It is only used when the rooms upstairs are full. I shut the door and lock it.

I cry for a long time – for myself, for the old woman with the bald head, for all the sadness of this damned world, for all the fools and all the defeated. . . .

In this fitting-room there is a dress in one of the cupboards which has been worn a lot by the mannequins and is going to be sold off for four hundred francs. The saleswoman has promised to keep it for me. I have tried it on; I have seen myself in it. It is a black dress with wide sleeves embroidered in vivid colours – red, green, blue, purple. It is my dress. If I had been wearing it I should never have stammered or been stupid.

Now I have stopped crying. Now I shall never have that dress. Today, this day, this hour, this minute I am utterly defeated. I have had enough.

Now the circle is complete. Now, strangely enough, I am no longer afraid of Mr Blank. He is one thing and I am another. He knew me right away, as soon as he came in at the door. And I knew him. . . .

I go into the other room, this time without knocking. Salvatini has gone. Mr Blank is still writing letters. Is he making dates with all the girls he knows in Paris? I bet that's what he is doing.

He looks at me with distaste. Plat du jour – boiled eyes, served cold. . . .

Well, let's argue this out, Mr Blank. You, who represent Society, have the right to pay me four hundred francs a month. That's my market value, for I am an inefficient member of Society, slow in the uptake, uncertain, slightly damaged in the fray, there's no denying it. So you have the right to pay me four hundred francs a month, to lodge me in a small, dark room, to clothe me shabbily, to harass me with worry and monotony and unsatisfied longings till you get me to the point when I blush at a look, cry at a word. We can't all be happy, we can't all be rich, we can't all be lucky – and it would be so much less fun if we were. Isn't it so, Mr Blank? There must be the dark background to show up the bright colours. Some must cry so that the others may be able to laugh the more heartily. Sacrifices are necessary. ... Let's say that you have this mystical right to cut my legs off. But the right to ridicule me afterwards because I am a cripple – no, that I think you haven't got. And that's the right you hold most dearly, isn't it? You must be able to despise the people you exploit. But I wish you a lot of trouble, Mr Blank, and just to start off with, your damned shop's going bust. Alleluia! Did I say all this? Of course I didn't. I didn't even think it.

I say that I'm ill and want to go. (Get it in first.) And he says he quite agrees that it would be the best thing. 'No regrets,' he says, 'no regrets.'

And there I am, out in the Avenue Marigny, with my month's pay – four hundred francs. And the air so sweet, as it can only be in Paris. It is autumn and the dry leaves are blowing along. Swing high, swing low, swing to and fro....

Thinking of my jobs....

There was that one I had in the shop called Young Britain. X plus Z B W. That meant fcs. 68·60. Then another hieroglyphic – X Q15tn – meant something else, fcs. 112·75. Little boys' sailor suits were there, and young gentlemen's Norfolk suits were there. ... Well, I got the sack from that in a week, and very pleased I was too.

Then there was that other job – as a guide. Standing in the middle of the Place de l'Opéra, losing my head and not knowing the way to the Rue de la Paix. North, south, east, west – they have no meaning for me. ... They want to saunter, this plump, placid lady and her slightly less placid daughter. They want to saunter in the beautiful Paris sunlight, to the Rue de la Paix.

I pull myself together and we get to the Rue de la Paix. We go to the French-English dress-shops and we go to the French-French dress-shops. And then they say they want to have lunch. I take them to a restaurant in the Place de la Madeleine. They are enormously rich, these two, the mother and the daughter. Both are very rich and very sad. Neither can imagine what it is like to be happy or even to be gay, neither the mother nor the daughter.

In the restaurant the waiter suggests pancakes with rum sauce for dessert. They are strict teetotallers, but they lap up the rum sauce. I've never seen anybody's mood change so quickly as the mother's did, after they had had two helpings of it.

'What delicious sauce!' They have a third helping. Their eyes are swimming. The daughter's eyes say 'Certainly, certainly'; the mother's eyes say 'Perhaps, perhaps....'

'It is strange how sad it can be – sunlight in the afternoon, don't you think?'

'Yes,' I say, 'it can be sad.'

But the softened mood doesn't last.

She has coffee and a glass of water and is herself again.

Now she wants to be taken to the exhibition of Loie Fuller materials, and she wants to be taken to the place where they sell that German camera which can't be got anywhere else outside Germany, and she wants to be taken to a place where she can buy a hat which will épater everybody she knows and yet be easy to wear, and on top of all this she wants to be taken to a certain exhibition of pictures. But she doesn't remember the man's name and she isn't sure where the exhibition is. However, she knows that she will recognize the name when she hears it.

I try. I question waiters, old ladies in lavabos, girls in shops. They all respond. There is a freemasonry among those who prey upon the rich. I manage everything, except perhaps the hat.

But she saw through me. She only gave me twenty

francs for a tip and I never got another job as a guide from the American Express. That was my first and last.

I try, but they always see through me. The passages will never lead anywhere, the doors will always be shut. I know....

Then I start thinking about the black dress, longing for it, madly, furiously. If I could get it everything would be different. Supposing I ask So-and-so to ask So-and-so to ask Madame Perron to keep it for me? ... I'll get the money. I'll get it....

Walking in the night with the dark houses over you, like monsters. If you have money and friends, houses are just houses with steps and a front-door – friendly houses where the door opens and somebody meets you, smiling. If you are quite secure and your roots are well struck in, they know. They stand back respectfully, waiting for the poor devil without any friends and without any money. Then they step forward, the waiting houses, to frown and crush. No hospitable doors, no lit windows, just frowning darkness. Frowning and leering and sneering, the houses, one after another. Tall cubes of darkness, with two lighted eyes at the top to sneer. And they know who to frown at. They know as well as the policeman on the corner, and don't you worry....

Walking in the night. Back to the hotel. Always the same hotel. You press the button. The door opens. You go up the stairs. Always the same stairs, always the same room....

The landing is empty and deserted. At this time of night there are no pails, no brooms, no piles of dirty sheets. The man next door has put his shoes outside – long, pointed, patent-leather shoes, very cracked. He does get dressed, then.... I wonder about this man. Perhaps he is a commercial traveller out of a job for the moment. Yes, that's what he might be – a commis voyageur. Perhaps he's a traveller in dressing-gowns.

Now, quiet, quiet. ... This is going to be a nice sane fortnight. 'Quiet, quiet,' I say to the clock when I am winding it up, and it makes a noise between a belch and a giggle.

*

The bathroom here is on the ground floor. I lie in the bath, listening to the patronne talking to a client. He says he wants a room for a young lady-friend of his. Not at once, he is just looking around.

'A room? A nice room?'

I watch cockroaches crawling from underneath the carpet and crawling back again. There is a flowered carpet in this bathroom, two old arm-chairs and a huge wardrobe with a spotted mirror.

'A nice room?' Of course, une belle chambre, the client wants. The patronne says she has a very beautiful room on the second floor, which will be vacant in about a month's time.

That's the way it is, that's the way it goes, that was the way it went. ... A room. A nice room. A beautiful room. A beautiful room with bath. A very beautiful room with bath. A bedroom and sitting-room with bath. Up to the dizzy heights of the suite. Two bedrooms, sitting-room, bath and vestibule. (The small bedroom is in case you don't feel like me, or in case you meet somebody you like better and come in late.) Anything you want brought up on the dinner-wagon. (But, alas! the waiter has a louse on his collar. What is that on his collar? ... Bitte schön, mein Herr, bitte schön. ...) Swing high. ... Now, slowly, down. A beautiful room with bath. A room with bath. A nice room. A room. ...

Now, what are they saying? 'Marthe, montrez le numéro douze.' And the price? Four hundred francs a month. I am paying three times as much as that for my room on the fourth floor. It shows that I have ended as a successful woman, anyway, however I may have started.

One look at me and the prices go up. And when the Exhibition is pulled down and the tourists have departed, where shall I be? In the other room, of course – the one just off the Gray's Inn Road, as usual trying to drink myself to death....

When I get upstairs the man next door is out on the landing, also yelling for Marthe. His flannel night-shirt scarcely reaches his knees. When he sees me he grins, comes to the head of the stairs and stands there, blocking the way.

'Bonjour. Ça va?'

I walk past him without answering and slam the door of my room. I expect all this is a joke. I expect he tells his friend on the floor below: 'An English tourist has taken the room next to mine. I have a lot of fun with that woman.'

A girl is making-up at an open window immediately opposite. The street is so narrow that we are face to face, so to speak. I can see socks, stockings and underclothes drying on a line in her room. She averts her eyes, her expression hardens. I realize that if I watch her making-up she will retaliate by staring at me when I do the same thing. I half-shut my window and move away from it. A terrible hotel, this – an awful place. I must get out of it. Only I would have landed here, only I would stay here....

I have just finished dressing when there is a knock on the door. It's the commis, in his beautiful dressing-gown, immaculately white, with long, wide, hanging sleeves. I wonder how he got hold of it. Some woman must have given it to him. He stands there smiling his silly smile. I stare at him. He looks like a priest, the priest of some obscene, half-understood religion.

At last I manage; 'Well, what is it? What do you want?'

'Nothing,' he says, 'nothing.'

'Oh, go away.'

He doesn't answer or move. He stands in the doorway, smiling. (Now then, you and I understand each other, don't we? Let's stop pretending.)

I put my hand on his chest, push him backwards and bang the door. It's quite easy. It's like pushing a paper man, a ghost, something that doesn't exist.

And there I am in this dim room with the bed for madame and the bed for monsieur and the narrow street outside (what they call an impasse), thinking of that white dressing-gown, like a priest's robes. Frightened as hell. A nightmare feeling....

This morning the hall smells like a very cheap Turkish bath in London – the sort of place that is got up to look respectable and clean outside, the passage very antiseptic and the woman who meets you a cross between a prison-wardress and a deaconess, and everybody speaking in whispering voices with lowered eyes: 'Foam or Turkish, madam?' And then you go down into the Turkish bath itself and into a fog of stale sweat – ten, twenty years old.

The patron, the patronne and the two maids are having their meal in a room behind the bureau. They have some friends with them. Loud talking and laughing. ... '"Tu n'oses pas," qu'elle m'a dit. "Ballot!" qu'elle m'a dit. Comment, je n'ose pas? Vous allez voir que je lui ai dit: "Attends, attends, ma fille. Tu vas voir si je n'ose pas." Alors, vous savez ce que j'ai fait? J'ai....'

His voice pursues me out into the street. 'Attends, ma fille, attends....'

I've got to find another hotel. I feel ill and giddy, I'd better take a taxi. Where to? I remember that I have an address in my handbag, a brochure with pictures. Le hall, le restaurant, le lounge, a bedroom with bath, a bedroom without bath, etcetera. Everything of the most respectable – that's the place for me....

There is a porter at the door and at the reception-desk a grey-haired woman and a sleek young man.

'I want a room for tonight.'

'A room? A room with bath?'

I am still feeling ill and giddy. I say confidentially, leaning forward: 'I want a light room.'

The young man lifts his eyebrows and stares at me.

I try again. 'I don't want a room looking on the courtyard. I want a light room.'

'A light room?' the lady says pensively. She turns over the pages of her books, looking for a light room.

'We have number 219,' she says. 'A beautiful room with bath. Seventy-five francs a night.' (God, I can't afford that.) 'It's a very beautiful room with bath. Two windows. Very light,' she says persuasively.

A girl is called to show me the room. As we are about to start for the lift, the young man says, speaking out of the side of his mouth: 'Of course you know that number 219 is occupied.'

'Oh no. Number 219 had his bill the day before yesterday,' the receptionist says. 'I remember. I gave it to him myself.'

I listen anxiously to this conversation. Suddenly I feel that I must have number 219, with bath – number 219, with rose-coloured curtains, carpet and bath. I shall exist on a different plane at once if I can get this room, if only for a couple of nights. It will be an omen. Who says you can't escape from your fate? I'll escape from mine, into room number 219. Just try me, just give me a chance.

'He asked for his bill,' the young man says, in a voice which is a triumph of scorn and cynicism. 'He asked for his bill but that doesn't mean that he has gone.'

The receptionist starts arguing. 'When people ask for their bills, it's because they are going, isn't it?'

'Yes,' he says, '*French* people. The others ask for their bills to see if we're going to cheat them.'

'My God,' says the receptionist, 'foreigners, foreigners, my God. . . .'

The young man turns his back, entirely dissociating himself from what is going on.

Number 219 – well, now I know all about him. All the time they are talking I am seeing him – his trousers, his shoes, the way he brushes his hair, the sort of girls he likes. His hand-luggage is light yellow and he has a paunch. But I can't see his face. He wears a mask, number 219....

'Show the lady number 334.'

The lady-like girl – we are all ladies here, all ladies – takes me up in the lift and shows me a comfortably furnished room which looks on to a high, blank wall.

'But I don't want a room looking on the courtyard. I want a light room.'

'This is a very light room,' the girl says, turning on the lamp by the bed.

'No,' I say. 'I mean a light room. A *light* one. Not a dark one.' She stares at me. I suppose I sound a bit crazy. I say: 'Yes.... Thank you very much – but no.'

The receptionist downstairs tries to stop me and argue about other rooms she has – beautiful rooms. I say: 'Yes, yes, I'll telephone,' and rush out.

A beautiful room with bath? A room with bath? A nice room? A room? ... But never tell the truth about this business of rooms, because it would bust the roof off everything and undermine the whole social system. All rooms are the same. All rooms have four walls, a door, a window or two, a bed, a chair and perhaps a bidet. A room is a place where you hide from the wolves outside and that's all any room is. Why should I worry about changing my room?

When I get back to the hotel after I have had something to eat, it looks all right and smells as respectable as you please. I imagined it all, I imagined everything.... Somebody's *Times Literary Supplement* peeps coyly from the letter-rack. A white-haired American lady and a girl who looks like her daughter are talking in the hall.

'Look here, look at this. Here's a portrait of Rimbaud. Rimbaud lived here, it says.'

'And here's Verlaine.... Did he live here too?'

'Yes, he lived here too. They both lived here. They lived here together. Well now, isn't that interesting?'

The commis is on the landing. He scowls at me and at once goes into his bedroom and shuts the door. Well, that's all right, that's all right. If we both try hard to avoid each other, we ought to be able to manage it.

The room welcomes me back.

'There you are,' it says. 'You didn't go off, then?'

'No, no. I thought better of it. Here I belong and here I'll stay.'

•

He always called that bar the Pig and Lily, because the proprietor's name was Pecanelli. It is in one of those streets at the back of the Montparnasse station. Got up to look like an olde English tavern. I don't see why I shouldn't revisit it. I have never made scenes there, collapsed, cried – so far as I know I have a perfectly clean slate. We used to go there, have a couple of drinks, eat hot dogs and talk about the next war or something like that. Nothing to cry about, I mean. . . .

'We?' Well, he was one of those people with very long, thin faces and very pale blue eyes. After working in a Manchester shipping-office until he was twenty-five, he had broken away and come to Paris, and was reading for his medical degree at the University. A loving relative supplied him with the money – that was one story. But another was that he really kept going on money he won at cards. That might have been true, for he was the sort that plays cards very well.

He loved popular fairs, this boy – the Neuilly fair, the Montmartre fair, even the merry-go-rounds at the Lion de Belfort – and he had painfully taught himself to like music. Bach, of course, was his favourite composer. The others, he said, he preferred to read, not to listen to. 'Heard melodies are sweet, but those unheard are sweeter'

– that sort of thing. He was a bit of a fish, really. Sometimes he made my blood run cold. And in spite of his long, thin face, he wasn't sensitive.

One day he said: 'I'll take you to see something rather interesting.' And, wandering along the streets at the back of the Halles, we came to a café where the clients paid for the right, not to have a drink, but to sleep. They sat close-pressed against each other with their arms on the tables, their heads in their arms. Every place in the room was filled; others lay along the floor. We squinted in at them through the windows. 'Would you like to go in and have a look at them?' he said, as if he were exhibiting a lot of monkeys. 'It's all right, we can go in – the chap here knows me. There's one fellow who is usually here. If you stand him a few drinks and get him really going he tries to eat his glass. It's very curious. You ought to see that.'

When I said: 'Not for anything on earth,' he thought I had gone shy or sentimental. 'Well,' I said, 'all right. I'll watch you eating a glass with pleasure.' He didn't like that at all.

I arrive thinking of this boy, and screw myself up to go into a room full of people. But the place is empty – dead as a door-nail. There is a new proprietor – a fat, bald man with a Dutch nose. He has only been here for two years, he tells me.

The speciality now is Javanese food, and the English hunting-scenes on the walls look very exotic. ... Tally-ho, tally-ho, tally-ho, a-hunting we will go. ... The cold, clear voices, the cold, light eyes. ... Tally-ho, tally-ho, tally-ho. ...

A party of three comes in – two men and a girl. One of the men stares at me. He says to the girl: 'Tu la connais, la vieille?'

Now, who is he talking about? Me? Impossible. Me – la vieille?

The girl says: 'The Englishwoman? No, I don't know her. Why should you imagine I know her?'

This is as I thought and worse than I thought. ... A mad old Englishwoman, wandering around Montparnasse. 'À Paris il y a des Anglaises, Oah, yes, oah, yes, Aussi plat's comm' des punaises, Oah, yes, oah, yes. ...' This is indeed worse than I thought.

I stare at the young man. He looks embarrassed and turns his eyes away. Not French. ...

This is indeed worse than I thought. That's what I was told when I came back to London that famous winter five years ago. 'Why didn't you drown yourself,' the old devil said, 'in the Seine?' In the Seine, I ask you – but that was just what he said. A very proper sentiment – but what a way to put it! Talk about being melodramatic! 'We consider you as dead. Why didn't you make a hole in the water? Why didn't you drown yourself in the Seine?' These phrases run trippingly off the tongues of the extremely respectable. They think in terms of a sentimental ballad. And that's what terrifies you about them. It isn't their cruelty, it isn't even their shrewdness – it's their extraordinary naiveté. Everything in their whole bloody world is a cliché. Everything is born out of a cliché, rests on a cliché, survives by a cliché. And they believe in the clichés – there's no hope.

Then the jam after the medicine. I shall receive a solicitor's letter every Tuesday containing £2 10*s*. 0*d*. A legacy, the capital not to be touched. ... 'Who?'

When I heard I was very surprised – I shouldn't have thought she liked me at all. 'You may consider yourself very fortunate,' he said, and when I saw the expression in his eyes I knew exactly why she did it. She did it to annoy the rest of the family. ... And of course it was impossible to tell me of this before, because they didn't know my address. There was nothing to say to that except: 'Goodbye, dear sir, and mind you don't trip over the hole in the carpet.'

It's so like him, I thought, that he refuses to call me

Sasha, or even Sophie. No, it's Sophia, full and grand. Why didn't you drown yourself in the Seine, Sophia? ... 'Sophia went down where the river flowed – Wild, wild Sophia. ...'

Well, that was the end of me, the real end. Two-pound-ten every Tuesday and a room off the Gray's Inn Road. Saved, rescued and with my place to hide in – what more did I want? I crept in and hid. The lid of the coffin shut down with a bang. Now I no longer wish to be loved, beautiful, happy or successful. I want one thing and one thing only – to be left alone. No more pawings, no more pryings – *leave me alone.* ... (They'll do that all right, my dear.)

'At first I was afraid they would let gates bang on my hindquarters, and I used to be nervous of unknown people and places.' Quotation from *The Autobiography of a Mare* – one of my favourite books. ... We English are so animal-conscious. We know so instinctively what the creatures feel and why they feel it. ...

It was then that I had the bright idea of drinking myself to death. Thirty-five pounds of the legacy had accumulated, it seemed. That ought to do the trick.

I did try it, too. I've had enough of these streets that sweat a cold, yellow slime, of hostile people, of crying myself to sleep every night. I've had enough of thinking, enough of remembering. Now whisky, rum, gin, sherry, vermouth, wine with the bottles labelled 'Dum vivimus, vivamus. ...' Drink, drink, drink. ... As soon as I sober up I start again. I have to force it down sometimes. You'd think I'd get delirium tremens or something.

Nothing. I must be solid as an oak. Except when I cry.

I watch my face gradually breaking up – cheeks puffing out, eyes getting smaller. Never mind. 'While we live, let us live,' say the bottles of wine. When we give, let us give. Besides, it isn't my face, this tortured and tormented mask. I can take it off whenever I like and hang it up on a nail. Or shall I place on it a tall hat with a green feather, hang a veil over the lot, and walk about the dark streets so merrily? Singing defiantly 'You don't like me, but I don't like you either. "Don't like jam, ham or lamb, and I *don't* like roly-poly. ..."' Singing 'One more river to cross, that's Jordan, Jordan....'

I have no pride – no pride, no name, no face, no country. I don't belong anywhere. Too sad, too sad. ... It doesn't matter, there I am, like one of those straws which floats round the edge of a whirlpool and is gradually sucked into the centre, the dead centre, where everything is stagnant, everything is calm. Two-pound-ten a week and a room just off the Gray's Inn Road....

All this time I am reading the menu over and over again. This used to be a place where you could only get hot dogs, choucroute, Vienna steak, Welsh rabbit and things like that. Now, it's more ambitious. 'Spécialités Javanaises (par personne, indivisibles): Rystafel complet (16 plats), 25.00, Rystafel petit (10 plats), 17.50, Nassi Goreng, 12.50. ...' The back of the menu is covered with sketches of little women and 'Send more money, send more money' is written over and over again. This amuses me. I think of all the telegraph-wires buzzing 'Send more money'. In spite of everything, the wires from Paris always buzzing 'Send more money'.

The three people at the next table are talking about horse-racing. The two men are Dutch.

I get a pencil out of my bag. I write in a corner of the menu 'As-tu compris? Si, j'ai compris. I hope you got that. Yes, I got it.' I fold the menu up and put it in my bag. A little souvenir....

The door opens. Five Chinese come in. They walk down to the end of the room in single file and stand there, talking. Then they all file solemnly out again, smiling politely. The proprietor mutters for a bit. Then he pretends to arrange the forks and knives on a table near by, and tells us that before they ordered drinks they wanted to see the fire lighted in the open grate, which is part of the olde English atmosphere. They wanted to see the flames dance. For a long time, he says, he has known that everybody in Montparnasse is mad, but this is the last straw. 'Tous piqués,' he says, with such an accent of despair, 'tous dingo, tous, tous, tous....'

I am not at all sad as I walk back to the hotel. When I remember how one well-directed 'Oh, my God,' lays me out flat in London, I can only marvel at the effect this place has on me. I expect it is because the drink is so much better.

No, I am not sad, but by the time I get to the Boulevard St Michel I am feeling tired. I have walked along here so often, feeling tired. ... Here is the fountain with the beautiful prancing horses. There is a tabac where I can have a drink near the next statue, the quinine statue.

Just then two men come up from behind and walk along on either side of me. One of them says: 'Pourquoi êtes-vous si triste?'

Yes, I am sad, sad as a circus-lioness, sad as an eagle without wings, sad as a violin with only one string and that one broken, sad as a woman who is growing old. Sad, sad, sad. ... Or perhaps if I just said 'merde' it would do as well.

I don't speak and we walk along in silence. Then I say: 'But I'm not sad. Why should you think I'm sad?' Is it a ritual? Am I bound to answer the same question in the same words?

We stop under a lamp-post to guess nationalities. So they say, though I expect it is because they want to have a closer look at me. They tactfully don't guess mine. Are they Germans? No. Scandinavians, perhaps? No, the shorter one says they are Russians. When I hear that I at once accept their offer to go and have a drink. Les Russes – that'll wind up the evening nicely....

There are two cafés opposite each other in this street near my hotel – the one where the proprietor is hostile, the one where the proprietor is neutral. I must be a bit drunk, because I lead them into the wrong one.

My life, which seems so simple and monotonous, is really a complicated affair of cafés where they like me and cafés where they don't, streets that are friendly, streets that aren't, rooms where I might be happy, rooms where I never shall be, looking-glasses I look nice in, looking-glasses I don't, dresses that will be lucky, dresses that won't, and so on.

However, being a bit tight, here I am on the wrong side of the street in the hostile café. Not that it matters, as I am not alone.

One of the Russians, the younger, is good-looking in a gentle, melancholy way. He is vaguely like the man who always took the spy-parts in German films some years ago. It's the shape of his head. The other is short and fair, with very blue eyes. He wears pince-nez. He must be the more alive of the two, because I find myself looking at him and talking to him all the time.

The usual conversation. ... I say that I am not sad. I tell them that I am very happy, very comfortable, quite rich enough, and that I am over here for two weeks to buy a lot of clothes to startle my friends – my many friends. The shorter man, who it seems is a doctor, is willing to believe that I am happy but not that I am rich. He has often noticed, he says, that Englishwomen have melancholy expressions. It doesn't mean anything. The other one is impressed by my fur coat, I can see. He is willing to believe that I am rich but he says again that he doesn't think I am happy. The short man must be the more worldly-wise; the other one is like me – he has his feelings and sticks to them. He is the one who accosted me.

'I feel a great sadness in you,' he says.

Tristesse, what a nice word! Tristesse, lointaine, langsam, forlorn, forlorn. ...

Now, for goodness' sake, listen to this conversation, which, after the second drink, seems to be about gods and goddesses.

'Madame Vénus se fâchera,' the short one is saying, wagging his finger at me.

'Oh, her!' I say. 'I don't like her any more. She's played me too many dirty tricks.'

'She does that to everyone. All the same, be careful. ... What god do they worship in England, what goddess?'

'I don't know, but it certainly isn't Venus. Somebody wrote once that they worship a bitch-goddess. It certainly isn't Venus.'

Then we talk about cruelty. I look into the distance with a blank expression and say: 'Human beings are cruel – horribly cruel.'

'Not at all,' the older one answers irritably, 'not at all. That's a very short-sighted view. Human beings are struggling, and so they are egotists. But it's wrong to say that they are wholly cruel – it's a deformed view.'

That goes on for a bit and then peters out. Now we have discussed love, we have discussed cruelty, and they sheer off politics. It's rather strange – the way they sheer off politics. Nothing more to be discussed.

Well, we'll meet again, shan't we? ... Of course we shall. It would be a pity not to meet again, wouldn't it? Will I meet them at the Pékin tomorrow for lunch? I have an idea that I shan't be feeling much like Chinese food at half-past twelve tomorrow. We arrange to meet at the Dôme at four o'clock.

They conduct me to the door of my hotel. The younger one remembers that I have left my menu behind – I had been showing it to them, the sketches of the little women and the 'Send more money, send more money' – and goes back to get it.

'Don't trouble. I don't really want it.'

But he has gone before I can stop him. I must keep this thing. It's fate.

Again I lie awake, trying to resist a great wish to go to a hairdresser in the morning to have my hair dyed.

*

When I come out of the hotel next morning a little old woman stops me and asks for money. I give her two francs. When she thanks me she looks straight into my eyes with an ironical expression.

As I go past the baker's shop at the corner of the street she comes out, with a long loaf of bread, smiles at me and waves gaily, I wave back. For a moment I escape from myself. But she disappears along a side-street, eating the loaf, and again I start thinking about dyeing my hair.

I pass the Italian restaurant. I pass Théodore's. It's a long way to the place I usually eat at. I hesitate, turn back, go in. I had meant to avoid Théodore's, because he might recognize me, because he might think I am changed, because he might say so.

I sit down in a corner, feeling uneasy.

He hasn't changed at all. He looks across the room at me from behind the bar and half-smiles. He has recognized me.... Very unlikely. Besides, what if he has, what's it matter? They can't kill you, can they? Oh, can't they, though, can't they?

Today I must be very careful, today I have left my armour at home.

Théodore's is more expensive than most of the restaurants round here and it is not very full. I watch the girl opposite cutting up the meat on her plate. She prongs a bit with her fork and puts it into her companion's mouth. He eats, registers pleasure as hard as he can, prods round for the best bit on his plate and feeds her with it. At any moment you expect these two to start flapping wings and chirping.

Then there's a middle-aged couple with their napkins tucked under their chins and a pretty woman accompanied by her husband – husband, I think, not lover.

These people all fling themselves at me. Because I am uneasy and sad they all fling themselves at me larger than life. But I can put my arm up to avoid the impact and they slide gently to the ground. Individualists, completely wrapped up in themselves, thank God. It's the extrovert, prancing around, dying for a bit of fun – that's the person you've got to be wary of.

I order sole and white wine. I eat with my eyes glued on my plate, the feeling of panic growing worse. (I told you not to come in here, I told you not to.)

At last, coffee. I wish I wasn't sitting so far from the door. However, it's nearly over. Soon I shall be out in the street again. I feel better.

I light a cigarette and drink the coffee slowly. As I am doing this two girls walk in – a tall, red-haired one and a little, plump, dark one. Sports clothes, no hats, English.

Théodore waddles up to their table and talks to them. The tall girl speaks French very well. I can't hear what Théodore is saying, but I watch his mouth moving and the huge moon-face under the tall chef's cap.

The girls turn and stare at me.

'Oh, my God!' the tall one says.

Théodore goes on talking. Then he too turns and looks at me. 'Ah, those were the days,' he says.

'Et qu'est-ce qu'elle fout ici, maintenant?' the tall girl says, loudly.

Now everybody in the room is staring at me; all the eyes in the room are fixed on me. It has happened.

I am calm, but my hand starts shaking so violently that I have to put the coffee-cup down.

'Everybody,' Théodore says, 'comes back to Paris. Always.' He retires behind the bar.

I make a great effort and look at the tall girl. She immediately turns her eyes away and starts talking about food – different ways of cooking chicken. The little one hangs on every word.

Her red hair is arranged so carefully over her tiny skull.

Her voice is hard and clear. Those voices like uniforms – tinny, meaningless. ... Those voices that they brandish like weapons.

But what language! Considering the general get-up what you should have said was: 'Qu'est-ce qu'elle fiche ici?' Considering the general get-up, surely that's what you should have said. What language, what language! What would Debenham & Freebody say, and what Harvey Nichols?

Well, everybody has had a good stare at me and a short, disapproving stare at the two girls, and everybody starts eating again.

'Ah! quelle plaie, quelle plaie, les Anglais,' as the old gentleman in the Cros de Cagnes bus said. But a plague that pays, my dear, a plague that pays. And merrily, merrily, life goes on. ... 'Quelle plaie, quelle plaie, les Anglais,' he said, sighing so deeply.

The waitress passes by my table and I ask for the bill.

'There is still some coffee left, madame. Will you have some more?' She smiles at me. Without waiting for me to answer, she pours what remains in the pot into my cup. She is sorry for me, she is trying to be kind.

My throat shuts up, my eyes sting. This is awful. Now I am going to cry. This is the worst. ... If I do that I shall really have to walk under a bus when I get outside.

I try to decide what colour I shall have my hair dyed, and hang on to that thought as you hang on to something when you are drowning. Shall I have it red? Shall I have it black? Now, black – that would be startling. Shall I have it blond cendré? But blond cendré, madame, is the most difficult of colours. It is very, very rarely, madame, that hair can be successfully dyed blond cendré. It's even harder on the hair than dyeing it platinum blonde. First it must be bleached, that is to say, its own colour must be taken out of it – and then it must be dyed, that is to say, another colour must be imposed on it. (Educated hair. ... And then, what?)

I finish the coffee, pay the bill and walk out. I would give all that's left of my life to be able to put out my tongue and say: 'One word to you,' as I pass that girl's table. I would give all the rest of my life to be able even to stare coldly at her. As it is, I can't speak to her, I can't even look at her. I just walk out.

Never mind. ... One day, quite suddenly, when you're not expecting it, I'll take a hammer from the folds of my dark cloak and crack your little skull like an egg-shell. Crack it will go, the egg-shell; out they will stream, the blood, the brains. One day, one day.... One day the fierce wolf that walks by my side will spring on you and rip your abominable guts out. One day, one day. ... Now, now, gently, quietly, quietly....

Théodore comes out from behind the bar and opens the door for me. He smiles, his pig-eyes twinkle. I can't make out whether his smile is malicious (that goes for me, too) or apologetic (he meant well), or only professional.

What about the programme for this afternoon? That's the thing – to have a plan and stick to it. First one thing and then another, and it'll all be over before you know where you are.

But my legs feel weak. What, defeated already? Surely not. ... No, not at all. But I think I'll cross the road and sit quietly in the Luxembourg Gardens for a while.

Piecing it together, arguing it out....

All that happened was this: Théodore probably said to the girl: 'I think there's a compatriot of yours over there,' and the girl said: 'Oh, my God!' And then Théodore probably said: 'I remember her. She used to come here a good deal some years ago. Ah, those were the days. ...' And this and that. And then the girl said: 'Qu'est-ce qu'elle fout ici?' partly because she didn't like the look of me and partly because she wanted to show how well she spoke French and partly because she thought that

Théodore's was her own particular discovery. (But, my dear good lady, Théodore's has been crawling with kindly Anglo-Saxons for the last fifteen years to my certain knowledge, and probably much longer than that.) And that's everything that happened, and why get in a state about it? ... But I'm not, I'm not. Can I help it if my heart beats, if my hands go cold?

I turn my chair round with its back to the pond where the children sail their boats. Now I can see nothing but the slender, straight trunks of trees. They look young, these trees. This is a gentle place – a gentle, formal place. It isn't sad here, it isn't even melancholy.

The attendant comes up and sells me a ticket. Now everything is legal. If anyone says: 'Qu'est-ce qu'elle fout ici?' I can show the ticket. This is legal. ... I feel safe, clutching it. I can stay here as long as I like, putting two and two together, quite calmly, with nobody to interfere with me.

Last night and today – it makes a pretty good sentence. ... Qu'est-ce qu'elle fout ici, la vieille? What the devil (translating it politely) is she doing here, that old woman? What is she doing here, the stranger, the alien, the old one? ... I quite agree too, quite. I have seen that in people's eyes all my life. I am asking myself all the time what the devil I am doing here. All the time.

Old people pass and shabby women, and every now and again a gay-looking one, painted, in a big fur coat. A man goes by, strutting like a cock, wheeling a big pram. He is buttoned very tightly into a black overcoat, his scarf carefully arranged under a blue chin. Then another man, who looks almost exactly like him, playing with a little girl who can only just walk. He is shouting at her: 'You have a drop on your nose.' The little girl runs away from him shrieking in delighted fright, and he runs after her, taking small, fussy steps. They disappear into the trees and I hear him still calling out: 'Come here, you have a drop on your nose, you have a drop on your nose....'

It's all right. I'm not unhappy. But I start thinking about that kitten.

This happened in London, and the kitten belonged to the couple in the flat above – a German hairdresser and his English wife. The kitten had an inferiority complex and persecution mania and nostalgie de la boue and all the rest. You could see it in her eyes, her terrible eyes, that knew her fate. She was very thin, scraggy and hunted, with those eyes that knew her fate. Well, all the male cats in the neighbourhood were on to her like one o'clock. She got a sore on her neck, and the sore on her neck got worse. 'Disgusting,' said the German hairdresser's English wife. 'She ought to be put away, that cat.' Then the kitten, feeling what was in the wind, came down into my room. She crouched against the wall, staring at me with those terrible eyes and with that big sore on the back of her neck. She wouldn't eat, she snarled at caresses. She just crouched in the corner of the room, staring at me. After a bit of this I couldn't stand it any longer and I shooed her out. Very reluctantly she went at first, with those eyes still staring at me. And then like an arrow through the door and down the stairs. I thought about her all the rest of that day and in the evening I said: 'I chased that unfortunate kitten out of my room. I'm worried about her. Is she all right?' 'Oh, haven't you heard?' they said. 'She got run over. Mrs Greiner was going to take her to the chemist's to be put away, and she ran right out into the street.' Right out into the street she shot and a merciful taxi went over her....

I look at myself in the glass of my handbag. I said I would meet the Russian at four o'clock at the Dôme. He is one of those people with bright blue eyes and what they call a firm tread. He is sure to be an optimist.

We'll sit in the Dôme and talk about sanity and normal human intercourse. He'll say: 'No, no, not cruelty – just egotism. They don't mean it.' He will explain just where

I'm wrong, just where the reasoning has tripped up. Perhaps. ...

There are hollows under my eyes. Sitting on the terrace of the Dôme, drinking Pernods and talking about sanity with enormous hollows under my eyes?

I hear a clock striking and count the strokes. It's four o'clock.

'No, thank you,' I think, 'I'm not going wandering into the Dôme looking like this – no, thank you.'

At once I feel a great regret. He might have said something to comfort me. ...

I am empty of everything. I am empty of everything but the thin, frail trunks of the trees and the thin, frail ghosts in my room. 'La tristesse vaut mieux que la joie.'

In the glass just now my eyes were like that kitten's eyes.

I sit without moving, not unhappy.

Now it's getting dark. Now the gates are shutting. (Qu'est-ce qu'elle fout ici, la vieille?)

Get up, get up. Eat, drink, walk, march. ... Pourquoi êtes-vous triste?

Tomorrow I must certainly go and have my hair dyed. I know exactly the man I'll go to. His name is Félix, but I'm not sure of the street. However, if I go to the Galeries Lafayette I can find my way from there.

When you go into the room Félix is seated at a desk. He has curly hair, a sensitive face, very nice hands. He wears a black velvet jacket. The complete artist – Antoine's only rival. In the window of his shop a large photograph with an inscription: 'To Monsieur Félix, who has kept my hair beautiful for so long – Adrienne.' There's no hope of getting Félix to attend to me, of course, but I may have a good assistant.

It's all right. Tomorrow I'll be pretty again, tomorrow I'll be happy again, tomorrow, tomorrow. ...

*

I get up into the room. I bolt the door. I lie down on the

bed with my face in the pillow. Now I can rest before I go out again. What do I care about anything when I can lie on the bed and pull the past over me like a blanket? Back, back, back. ...

... I had just come up the stairs and I had to go down them again.

'No, no, your room's not ready. You must come back, come back. Come back between five and six.' 'What time is it now?' 'It's half-past ten.'

'Courage, courage, ma petite dame,' she says. 'Everything will go well.'

I go down the stairs again, clutching the banisters, step by step.

I stop a taxi. The man looks at me and hesitates. Perhaps he is afraid I may have my baby in his nice new taxi. What a thing to happen!

No danger at all, I want to say. Hours and hours and hours yet, she says.

I get back to the hotel and climb upstairs to my room. This is a hard thing to do. Has anybody ever had to do this before? Of course, lots of people – poor people. Oh, I see, of course, poor people. ... Still, it is a hard thing to do, walking around when you're like this. And half-past five is a long time off – centuries of time.

When I climb the stairs again I am not seeing so well.

'Courage, my little lady. Your room is ready now.'

A room, a bed where I can lie down. Now the worst is surely over. But the long night, the interminable night. ...

'Courage, courage,' she says. 'All will be well. All is going beautifully.'

This is a funny house. There are people having babies all over the place. Anyhow, at least two are having babies.

'Jesus, Jesus,' says one woman. 'Mother, Mother,' says another.

I do not speak. How long is it before I speak?

'Chloroform, chloroform,' I say when I speak. Of course I would. What nonsense! There is no doctor to give chloroform here. This is a place for poor people. Besides, she doesn't approve of chloroform. No Jesus, no Mother, and no chloroform either. . . .

What then?

This.

Always?

Yes, always.

She comes and wipes my forehead. She speaks to me in a language that is no language. But I understand it.

Back, back, back. . . . This has happened many times.

What are you? I am an instrument, something to be made use of. . . .

She darts from one room to another, encouraging, soothing, reproaching. 'Now, you're not trying. Courage, courage.' Speaking her old, old language of words that are not words.

A rum life, when you come to think of it. I'd hate to live it. However, to her it is just life. . . .

Afterwards I couldn't sleep. I would sleep for an hour or two, and then wake up and think about money, money, money for my son; money, money. . . .

Do I love him? Poor little devil, I don't know if I love him.

But the thought that they will crush him because we have no money – that is torture.

Money, money for my son, my beautiful son. . . .

I can't sleep. My breasts dry up, my mouth is dry. I can't sleep. Money, money. . . .

'Why!' she says. 'Can't you sleep? This will never do, never do.'

She probably knows why I can't sleep. I bet some of the others here can't either. Worrying about the same thing. (This is not *a* child; this is *my* child. Money, money. . . .)

'Well, why can't you sleep?' she says. 'Does he cry, this young man?'

'No, he hardly cries at all. Is it a bad sign, that he doesn't cry?'

'Why no, not at all. A beautiful, beautiful baby. ... But why can't you sleep?'

She has slanting eyes, very clear. I like people with clear, slanting eyes. I can still give myself up to people I like. (Tell me what to do. Have you a solution? Tell me what to do.)

She pats me on the shoulder and says: 'You're worrying about nothing at all. Everything will come right for you. I'll send you in a tisane of orange-flower water, and to-night you must sleep, sleep....'

I can't feed this unfortunate baby. He is taken out and given Nestlé's milk. So, I can sleep....

The next day she comes in and says: 'Now I am going to arrange that you will be just like what you were before. There will be no trace, no mark, nothing.'

That, it seems, is her solution.

She swathes me up in very tight, very uncomfortable bandages. Intricately she rolls them and ties them. She gives me to understand that this is usually an extra. She charges a great deal for this as a rule.

'I do this better than anyone in the whole of Paris,' she says. 'Better than any doctor, better than any of these people who advertise, better than anyone in the whole of Paris.'

And there I lie in these damned bandages for a week. And there he lies, swathed up too, like a little mummy. And never crying.

But now I like taking him in my arms and looking at him. A lovely forehead, incredibly white, the eyebrows drawn very faintly in gold dust....

Well, this was a funny time. (The big bowl of coffee in the morning with a pattern of red and blue flowers. I was always so thirsty.) But uneasy, uneasy.... Ought a baby to be as pretty as this, as pale as this, as silent as this? The other babies yell from morning to night. Uneasy....

When I complain about the bandages she says: 'I promise you that when you take them off you'll be just as you were before.' And it is true. When she takes them off there is not one line, not one wrinkle, not one crease.

And five weeks afterwards there I am, with not one line, not one wrinkle, not one crease.

And there he is, lying with a ticket tied round his wrist because he died in a hospital. And there I am looking down at him, without one line, without one wrinkle, without one crease....

•

The hairdresser also ends by calling me 'Ma petite dame'.

He reflects for some time about my hair, feels it between his fingers. Then: 'In your place, madame, I shouldn't hesitate. But not for a moment. A nice blond cendré,' he says.

That was just the right way to put it. 'If I were in your place, madame, I shouldn't hesitate.'

He touches my hair gently. The smell of soap, scent, hair lotion, the sound of the dryer in the next cubicle, his fingers touching my hair – I could go to sleep.

'Very well,' I say in a sulky voice. (At it again, dearie, at it again!)

Of course I can't look on at this operation. I read magazines – *Féminas, Illustrations, Eves.* Then I start in on the *Hairdresser*, the *Art of Hairdressing*, the *Hairdresser's Weekly* and a curious journal with a large section called 'the Hive' – answers to correspondents.

'*Pierrette Clair de la Lune* – No, mademoiselle, your letter is nonsensical. You will never get thin that way – never. Life is not so easy. Life, mademoiselle, is difficult. At your age it will be very difficult to get thin. But....

'*Petite Maman* – No, Petite Maman, you are not reasonable. Love is one thing; marriage – alas! – is quite another. If you haven't found that out yet you soon will, I assure you. Nevertheless....'

No, mademoiselle, no, madame, life is not easy. Do not delude yourselves. Nothing is easy. But there is hope (turn to page 5), and yet more hope (turn to page 9)....

I am in the middle of a long article by a lady who has had her breasts lifted when he takes the dryer off my head.

'Voilà,' he says....

'Yes,' he says, 'a very good blond cendré. A success.'

I had expected to think about this damned hair of mine without any let-up for days. (Is it all right? Is it not all right?) But before the taxi has got back to Montparnasse I have forgotten all about it.

I don't want to eat. I decide to go into the Luxembourg Gardens and sit there as I did yesterday. It's curious how peaceful I feel – as if I were possessed by something. Not that way – this way. Not up that street – this street. Just dance, and leave the music to me.... Like that.

There are some fish in the pool of the Médicis fountain. Three are red and one gold. The four fish look so forlorn that I wonder whether they are just starting them, or whether they have had a lot, and they have died off.

I stand for a long time, watching the fish. And several people who pass stop and also watch them. We stand in a row, watching the fish.

*

I must go and buy a hat this afternoon, I think, and tomorrow a dress. I must get on with the transformation act. But there I sit, watching the same procession of shabby women wheeling prams, of men tightly buttoned up into black overcoats.

One of the figures detaches itself from the procession and comes towards me. It is only when he is close to me and puts his hand out that I recognize him. The younger Russian, the melancholy one.

He also is tightly buttoned into a black overcoat. His scarf is carefully tied. He is wearing a black felt hat. Just like all the fathers attending the prams. Very correct, very respectable. He bows and shakes hands.

'You allow me?' He brings a chair close up to mine.

'You didn't go to meet my friend yesterday afternoon,' he says. 'No, I'm sorry, but I wasn't feeling well.' 'He was angry. He thought it wasn't at all nice of you. He said –' He starts to laugh. 'Well, what did he say?' 'Oh, he was in a bad temper. He had an annoying letter this morning.' 'I was vexed with myself,' I say, 'but I couldn't go.'

He says, not taking his eyes from mine: 'When I make an appointment I always keep it, even though I think the other person won't be there.' 'Do you? That's not my idea of a Russian at all.' 'Oh, Russians, Russians – why do you think they are so different from other people?'

He comes from the Ukraine, he tells me, and it's very hot there, and very cold in the winter. But again he slides away from the subject of Russia and everything Russian, though in other ways he is communicative about himself. He is a naturalized Frenchman and he has done his military service in France. He says his name is Nicolas Delmar, which doesn't sound very Russian to me. Anyway, that's what he calls himself, and he writes it on a bit of *Le Journal*, with his address, and gives it to me. He lives in Montrouge. He has some female relative – sister, mother, aunt, I can't make out – who is ill, which makes him very sad.

'But I can forget it,' he says. 'Every day I come up to the Quartier Latin, or I walk in the Luxembourg Gardens. I can forget it.'

He speaks French slowly and ponderously. This gives me confidence. Off we go into a full blast of philosophical discussion.

He says: 'For me, you see, I look at life like this: If

someone had come to me and asked me if I wished to be born I think I should have answered No. I'm sure I should have answered No. But no one asked me. I am here not through my will. Most things that happen to me – they are not my will either. And so that's what I say to myself all the time: "You didn't ask to be born, you didn't make the world as it is, you didn't make yourself as you are. Why torment yourself? Why not take life just as it comes? You have the right to; you are not one of the guilty ones." When you aren't rich or strong or powerful, you are not a guilty one. And you have the right to take life just as it comes and to be as happy as you can.'

While he is talking I have a strange idea that perhaps it is like that. . . . Now then, you, X – you must go down and be born. Oh, not me, please, not me. Well then, you, Y, you go along and be born – somebody's got to be. Where's Y? Y is hiding. Well, come on Z, you've got to go and be born. Come on, hurry up, hurry up. . . . There's one every minute. Or is it every second?

'But don't you ever wish to be rich or strong or powerful?'

'No longer,' he says, 'no longer. I prefer to be as I am. As things are now, I wouldn't wish to be rich or strong or powerful. I wouldn't wish to be one of the guilty ones. I know I am not guilty, so I have the right to be just as happy as I can make myself.'

We go on in this strain for some time. I wonder what on earth he does, what he is. He looks like a person who is living on a very small fixed income. As I am thinking this he tells me that he loves this part of Paris, the Quartier Latin, because he loves youth. I look very hard at him when he says this. But he just means that he loves youth.

'Yes,' I say. 'I love youth too. Who doesn't? And this is just the place, full of prams, babies and so forth.'

'I very seldom go to Montmartre,' he says. 'I very seldom go anywhere else. This is the part of Paris that I like – the Quartier Latin and Montparnasse.'

'Side by side and oh, so different.'

'Have you ever noticed,' he says, 'that when you go from one part of Paris to another, it's just like going from one town to another – even from one country to another? The people are different, the atmosphere is different, even the women dress differently.'

I don't know why I don't quite like him. This gentle, resigned melancholy – it seems unnatural in a man who can't be much over thirty, if so much as that. Or perhaps it is because he seems more the echo of a thing than the thing itself. One moment I feel this, and another I like him very much, as if he were the brother I never had.

I say: 'Montparnasse is very changed since I knew it first, I can tell you. That was just after the war,' I say recklessly. (As you love youth so much, that'll give you something to think about.)

'You came here just after the war?'

'Yes, and I lived here up to five years ago. Then I went back to England.'

'Yes, it must be very changed, very changed,' he says, pursing his lips and nodding his head.

'Oh, terrible,' I say. 'But I don't believe things change much really; you only think they do. It seems to me that things repeat themselves over and over again.'

He says: 'I think you are getting cold, madame. You are shivering. Would you like to go to a pâtisserie and have a cup of chocolate? There is a nice one near here.'

I say: 'I'd much rather go to a café and have a drink.'

I have an idea that he disapproves of this, but he says: 'Yes, certainly. Let's go.'

I make no mistake this time. We go to the neutral café.

When we are in a corner with a coffee and a *fine* each he says: 'Do you know what I feel about you? I think you are very lonely. I know, because for a long time I was lonely myself. I hated people, I didn't want to see anyone. And then one day I thought: "No, this isn't the way." And now I go about a lot. I force myself to. I have a lot of friends; I'm never alone. Now I'm much happier.'

That sounds pretty simple. I must try it when I get back to London. ...

I say: 'I liked your friend the other night.'

'Ah, yes,' he says, shaking his head. 'But he was vexed, and he's had bad news. ...' (The optimist hasn't any more use for me, I can see that.) 'But I have many friends. I'll introduce you to all of them if you wish. Will you allow me? Then you will never be alone and you'll be much happier, you'll see.'

'But do you think they'd like me, your friends?'

'But certainly. Absolutely yes.'

This young man is very comforting – almost as comforting as the hairdresser.

'Will you come along now and see a friend of mine? He's a painter. I think he is a man you'd like. He's always gay and he knows how to talk to everybody. ... Yes, Serge understands everybody – it's extraordinary.' (And, whether prince or prostitute, he always did his best. ...) 'Mais au fond, vous savez, il s'en fiche de tout, il s'en fiche de tout le monde.'

He sounds fine.

'Yes, I'd like to,' I say. 'But I can't this afternoon. I have to go and buy a hat.'

'Well, would you like to come tomorrow?' he says, and we arrange to meet at four o'clock the next day.

There used to be a good hat-shop in the Rue Vavin.

It doesn't exist any longer. I wander aimlessly along a lot of back streets where there aren't any hat-shops at all. And then a street that is alive with them – Virginie, Josette, Claudine. ... I look at the window of the first shop. There is a customer inside. Her hair, half-dyed, half-grey, is very dishevelled. As I watch she puts on a hat, makes a face at herself in the glass, and takes it off very quickly. She tries another – then another. Her expression is terrible – hungry, despairing, hopeful, quite crazy. At any moment you expect her to start laughing the laugh of the mad.

I stand outside, watching. I can't move. Hat after hat she puts on, makes that face at herself in the glass and throws it off again. Watching her, am I watching myself as I shall become? In five years' time, in six years' time, shall I be like that?

But she is better than the other one, the smug, white, fat, black-haired one who is offering the hats with a calm, mocking expression. You can almost see her tongue rolling round and round inside her cheek. It's like watching the devil with a damned soul. If I must end like one or the other, may I end like the hag.

I realize that I can't stay gaping in on them any longer and move off, very much shaken. Then I remember the Russian saying: 'I didn't ask to be born; I didn't make the world as it is; I didn't make myself as I am; I am not one of the guilty ones. And so I have a right to. . . .' Etcetera.

There are at least ten milliners' shops in this street. I decide to go into the last but one on the left-hand side and hope to strike lucky.

The girl in the shop says: 'The hats now are very difficult, very difficult. All my clients say that the hats now are very difficult to wear.'

This is a much larger shop than the other one. There is a cruel, crude light over the two mirrors and behind a long room stretching into dimness.

She disappears into the dimness and comes back with hat after hat, hat after hat, murmuring: 'All my clients are complaining that the hats now are very difficult to wear, but I think – I am sure – I shall manage to suit you.'

In the glass it seems to me that I have the same demented expression as the woman up the street.

'My God, not that one.'

I stare suspiciously at her in the glass. Is she laughing at me? No, I think not. I think she has the expression of someone whose pride is engaged. She is determined that before I go out of the shop I shall admit that she can make hats. As soon as I see this expression in her eyes I decide to trust her. I too become quite calm.

'You know, I'm bewildered. Please tell me which one I ought to have.'

'The first one I showed you,' she says at once.

'Oh, my God, not that one.'

'Or perhaps the third one.'

When I put on the third one she says: 'I don't want to insist, but yes – that is your hat.'

I look at it doubtfully and she watches me – not mockingly, but anxiously.

She says: 'Walk up and down the room in it. See whether you feel happy in it. See whether you'll get accustomed to it.'

There is no one else in the shop. It is quite dark outside. We are alone, celebrating this extraordinary ritual.

She says: 'I very seldom insist, but I am sure that when you have got accustomed to that hat you won't regret it. You will realize that it's your hat.'

I have made up my mind to trust this girl, and I must trust her.

'I don't like it much, but it seems to be the only one,' I say in a surly voice.

I have been nearly two hours in the shop, but her eyes are still quite friendly.

I pay for the hat. I put it on. I have a great desire to ask her to come and dine with me, but I daren't do it. All my spontaneity has gone. (Did I ever have any? Yes, I think sometimes I had – in flashes. Anyway, it's gone now. If I asked her to dine with me, it would only be a failure.)

She adjusts the hat very carefully. 'Remember, it must be worn forward and very much on one side. Comme ça.'

She sees me out, still smiling. A strange client, l'étrangère. ... The last thing she says is: 'All the hats now are very difficult. All my clients are complaining.'

I feel saner and happier after this. I go to a restaurant near by and eat a large meal, at the same time carefully watching the effect of the hat on the other people in the room, comme ça. Nobody stares at me, which I think is a good sign.

A man sitting near by asks if he may look at my evening paper, as he wants to go to the cinema tonight. Then he tries to start a conversation with me. I think: 'That's all right. ...'

*

When I go out into the Place de l'Odéon I am feeling happy, what with my new hair and my new hat and the good meal and the wine and the *fine* and the coffee and the smell of night in Paris. I'm not going to any beastly little bar tonight. No, tonight I'm going somewhere where there's music; somewhere where I can be with a lot of people; somewhere where there's dancing. But where? By myself, where can I go? I'll have one more drink first and then think it out.

Not the Dôme. I'll avoid the damned Dôme. And, of course, it's the Dôme I go to.

The terrace is crowded, but there are not many people inside. What on earth have I come in here for? I have always disliked the place, except right at the start, when the plush wasn't so resplendent and everybody spat on the floor. It was rather nice then.

I pay for my drink and go out. I am waiting to cross the street. Someone says: 'Excuse me, but can I speak to you? I think you speak English.'

I don't answer. We cross side by side.

He says: 'Please allow me to speak to you. I wish to so much.'

He speaks English with a very slight accent. I can't place it. I look at him and recognize him. He was sitting at a table in the corner opposite to mine at the Dôme.

'Please. Couldn't we go to a café and talk?'

'Of course,' I say. 'Why not?'

'Well, where shall we go?' he says in a fussy voice. 'You see, I don't know Paris well. I only arrived last night.'

'Oh?' I say.

As we walk along, I look sideways at him and can't make him out. He isn't trying to size me up, as they usually do – he is exhibiting himself, his own person. He is very good-looking, I noticed that in the Dôme. But the nervousness, the slightly affected laugh....

Of course. I've got it. Oh Lord, is that what I look like? Do I really look like a wealthy dame trotting round Montparnasse in the hope of –? After all the trouble I've gone to, is that what I look like? I suppose I do.

Shall I tell him to go to hell? But after all, I think, this is where I might be able to get some of my own back. You talk to them, you pretend to sympathize; then, just at the moment when they are not expecting it, you say: 'Go to hell.'

We are passing the Closerie des Lilas. He says: 'This looks a nice café. Couldn't we go in here?'

'All right. But it's very full. Let's sit on the terrace.'

The terrace is cold and dark and there is not another soul there.

'What about a drink?'

'You'll have to get hold of the waiter. He won't come out here.'

'I'll get him.'

He goes into the café and comes back with the waiter and two brandies.

He says: 'Have you ever felt like this – as if you can't bear any more, as if you must speak to someone, as if you must tell someone everything or otherwise you'll die?'

'I can imagine it.'

He is not looking at me – he hasn't looked at me once. He is looking straight ahead, gathering himself up for some effort. He is going to say his piece. I have done this so often myself that it is amusing to watch somebody else doing it.

'But why do you want to talk to me?'

He is going to say: 'Because you look so kind,' or 'Because you look so beautiful and kind,' or, subtly, 'Because you look as if you'll understand. . . .'

He says: 'Because I think you won't betray me.'

I had meant to get this man to talk to me and tell me all about it, and then be so devastatingly English that perhaps I should manage to hurt him a little in return for all the many times I've been hurt. . . . 'Because I think you won't betray me, because I think you won't betray me. . . .' Now it won't be so easy.

'Of course I won't betray you. Why should I betray you?'

'No,' he says. 'Why?'

He throws back his head and laughs. That's the gesture for showing off the teeth. Also, I suppose he is laughing at the idea of my being able to betray him.

'Very nice, very nice indeed. Beautiful teeth,' I say in an insolent voice.

'Yes, I know,' he answers simply.

But I have jarred him a bit. He finishes his drink and starts again.

'I am what they call in French a mauvais garçon.'

'But I like them. I like les mauvais garçons.'

For the first time he looks straight at me. He doesn't look away again, but goes on in the same nervous voice: 'I got into bad trouble at home. I ran away.'

'I am a Canadian, a French-Canadian,' he says.

'French-Canadian? I see.'

'Shall we have another drink?'

Again he has to go inside the café to fetch the waiter and the drinks. Now it's creeping into me, the brandy, creeping into my arms, my legs, making me feel hazy.

I listen to his story, which is that he joined the Foreign Legion, was in Morocco for three years, found it impossible to bear any longer, and escaped through Spain – Franco Spain. Just escaped from the Foreign Legion. ... La Légion, La Légion Étrangère. ...

'I had enormous luck, or I couldn't have done it. I got to Paris last night. I'm at a hotel near the Gare d'Orsay.'

'Is it as bad as they say, the Legion?'

'Oh, they tell a lot of lies about it. But I'd had enough. ... You don't believe me, do you? You don't believe anything I'm telling you. But it's always when a thing sounds not true that it is true,' he says.

Of course. I know that. ... You imagine the carefully-pruned, shaped thing that is presented to you is truth. That is just what it isn't. The truth is improbable, the truth is fantastic; it's in what you think is a distorting mirror that you see the truth.

'I'll tell you one thing I don't believe. I don't believe you're a French-Canadian.'

'Then what do you think I am?'

'Spanish? Spanish-American?'

He blinks and says to himself: 'Elle n'est pas si bête que ça.' Well, that might mean anything.

'It's awfully cold here,' I say, 'too cold to stay any longer.'

'No, please. Please don't go, you mustn't go. Or, if you wish, let's go somewhere else. But I must talk to you.'

His voice is so urgent that I begin to feel exasperated.

'But, my dear friend, I don't know what you think I can do. People who are in trouble want someone with money to help them. Isn't it so? Well, I haven't got any money.'

The corners of his mouth go down. They all say that.

I want to shout at him 'I haven't got any money, I tell you. I know what you're judging by. You're judging by my coat. You oughtn't to judge by my coat. You ought to judge by what I have on under my coat, by my handbag, by my expression, by anything you like. Not by this damned coat, which was a present – and the only reason I haven't sold it long ago is because I don't want to offend the person who gave it to me, and because if you knew what you really get when you try to sell things it would give you a shock, and because –'

Well, there you are – no use arguing. I can see he has it firmly fixed in his head that I'm a rich bitch and that if he goes on long enough I can be persuaded to part.

'But it isn't money I want,' he says. 'Really it isn't money. What I hoped was that we could go somewhere where we could be quite alone. I want to put my head on your breast and put my arms round you and tell you everything. You know, it's strange, but that's how I feel tonight. I could die for that – a woman who would put her arms round me and to whom I could tell everything. Couldn't we go somewhere like that?'

'No, we can't,' I say. 'Impossible.'

'Well,' he says, accepting this calmly, 'if you won't do that, I thought perhaps you could help me about my papers. You see, I have no papers, no passport. That's just why I'm in trouble. The slightest accident and I'm finished. I have no papers. But if I could get a passport, I would go to London. I'd be safe there. I could get in touch with friends.'

I say: 'And you think I can help you to get a passport? I? Me? But who do you think I am? This must be one of my good nights.'

At this moment I find everything so funny that I start laughing loudly. He laughs too.

'I can't stay on this damned terrace any longer. It's too cold.'

He raps on the window and, when the waiter comes, pays for the drinks.

'Now, where shall we go?' He puts his arm through mine and says, in French: 'Now, where?'

Well, what harm can he do to me? He is out for money and I haven't got any. I am invulnerable.

There we are, arm in arm, outside the Closerie des Lilas and when I think of my life it seems to me so comical that I have to laugh. It has taken me a long time to see how comical it has been, but I see it now, I do.

'You must tell me where to go,' he says, 'because I don't know Paris.'

I take him to the café where I go most nights – the place that is always empty. This is the first time that I have seen him in the bright light, close by. It is also the first time that, on these occasions, I haven't cared in the least what the man thinks of me, and am only curious to see what he looks like.

He doesn't look like a gigolo – not my idea of a gigolo at all. For instance, his hair is rather untidy. But, nice hair.

Another brandy-and-soda. I suppose all this money that he is spending on me is the sprat to catch a whale.

The waiter, giving him change, brings out of his pocket the most extraordinary collection of small money. Pieces of twenty-five centimes, of ten, of five – the table is covered with them. When he has slowly collected it all once more, he goes into the corner of the room, takes off his shoes and starts cleaning them.

I say: 'This is my sort of place – this chic, gay place. Do you like it?'

'No, I don't like it, but I understand why you come here. I'm not always so fond of human beings, either.'

Well, here's another who isn't as stupid as all that.

He says: 'You know, that waiter – he was quite sure we loved each other and were going to be very happy tonight. He was envying us.'

'Yes, I expect he'll stay awake all night thinking of it. Like hell he will.'

He looks disconsolate, tired, as if he were thinking: 'No good. Everything's got to be started all over again.' Poor gigolo!

I say: 'About your papers – there are people here who sell false passports. It can be done.'

'I know. I'm in touch with somebody already.'

'What, and you only got here last night! You haven't wasted much time.'

'No, and I'd better not, either.'

He is in some sort of trouble. I know that look. I want very much to comfort him – to say something to cheer him up.

'I like les mauvais garçons,' I say. He smiles. 'I know exactly what you want,' I say. 'You want somebody very rich and very chic.'

'Yes,' he says, 'yes, that's what would just suit me. And beautiful.'

'But, my dear, you're not going to find that at the Dôme.'

'Where shall I go, then? Where shall I find all that?'

'Ritz Bar,' I say vaguely.

After this I start my piece. I tell him my name, my address, everything. He says his name is René, and leaves it at that. I say I am sick of my hotel and want to leave it and find a flat or a studio.

He is on the alert at once. 'A studio? I think I could get you exactly the place you want.'

I am not so drunk as all that.

'I thought you said you'd just escaped from the Foreign Legion and only got to Paris last night and were going away again as soon as you could.'

'Why should that prevent me from trying to get you a studio if you want one?'

(Let it pass, dearie, let it pass. What's the matter?)

'Can I take you back to your hotel?'

'Yes, but it's too far to walk. I want a taxi.'

We sit in the taxi in silence. At the corner of the street we get out. I let him pay. (So much the worse for you. That will teach you to size up your types a bit better.)

'Let's have one more drink,' he says.

We walk up the street, trying to find a place that is open. Everything seems to be shut; it is past twelve. We go along the Rue St Jacques hand in hand. I am no longer self-conscious. Hand in hand we walk along, swinging our arms. Suddenly he stops, pulls me under a lamp-post and stares at me. The street is empty, the lights in the bars are out.

'Hey, isn't it a bit late in the day to do this?'

He says: 'Mais c'est complètement fou. It's hallucinating. Walking along here with you, I have the feeling that I'm with a –'

'With a *beau*-tiful young girl?'

'No,' he says. 'With a child.'

Now I have had enough to drink, now the moment of tears is very near. I say: 'Well, nothing's open. Everything's shut. I'm going home.'

He looks up at the door of my hotel.

'Can I come up to your room?'

'No, you can't.'

'Well, can I come back in a little while and get a room here myself and then come to see you?'

(The patronne saying: 'L'Anglaise has picked up someone. Have you seen?')

'No, don't come here. I shall be awfully vexed if you come here. Please don't.'

'Of course I won't if you ask me not to,' he says. Tactful. 'What about the hotel next door? Perhaps I could get a room there.'

The hotel next door? No, the hotel five or six doors off. That's the one. In that hotel there is a room with the biggest bed I have ever known – the biggest bed in the world, the bed of beds. ... Everything in the room is red. And there is nothing in it but this huge bed and a wash-stand and a bidet. Shall I go and lie on it again tonight, when everything is a caricature, a grimace?

I say: 'Well, I shouldn't if I were you. The hotels in this street – they look all right by this light, but they're not so comfortable. Try something more modern.'

'Rien à faire?'

'Rien à faire.'

He shrugs his shoulders. 'I'm sorry,' he says. ... 'What's this street? How can I get to the Boulevard St Michel?'

I don't believe in this pose of being a stranger to Paris, but he is certainly keeping it up pretty well.

Somebody is hammering at the door. I have bolted it – unnecessarily, as it can't be opened from the outside without a key.

Marthe says: 'You're wanted on the telephone. It's not very convenient when you bolt the door.'

I expect she has been trying to get in for some time.

I have a headache and feel very bad-tempered. I think: 'It's that man, of course. He's made up his mind that he's going to get some money out of me and "Vénus toute entière à sa proie attachée," isn't in it.'

While I am thinking this I am putting on my dressing-gown. I comb my hair without daring to look at myself in the glass.

I get downstairs to the telephone. There is nobody on the line.

'There was a monsieur,' the patronne says.

There was a monsieur, but the monsieur has gone.

I feel ill today. This would be an awful place to be ill in. They wouldn't even get me another bottle of Evian when the first was finished – they wouldn't do a thing.

I expect if I rang the bell and said that they must change the sheets they would do it. That's my idea of luxury – to have the sheets changed every day and twice on Sundays. That's my idea of the power of money.

Yes, I'll have the sheets changed. I'll lie in bed all day, pull the curtains and shut the damned world out. ... There was a monsieur, but the monsieur has gone. There was more than one monsieur, but they have all gone. What an assortment! One of every kind. ...

I'll lie in bed all day, pull the curtains and shut the damned world out.

Part Two

All the same, at three o'clock I am dressing to meet the Russian.

He is waiting. He says his friend Serge is expecting us. 'Le peintre,' he calls him.

I suggest taking a taxi but he seems horrified at the idea.

'No, no. We'll go by bus. It's quite near. It's only a few minutes away.' 'Couldn't we walk, then?' 'Oh yes, we could walk. It's just off the Avenue d'Orléans, about five minutes' walk.' 'It's more than five minutes,' I argue. 'It's more like half an hour.'

Soon now it will be winter. There are hardly any leaves on the trees and the man outside the Luxembourg Gardens is selling roast chestnuts.

We stand at the end of a long queue. No bus.

'Do let's take a taxi.' 'Very well. If you like,' he says unwillingly. 'But the man will be very vexed at having to go such a short distance. – Place Denfert-Rochereau, the Métro,' he says to the driver. – 'It won't be far to walk from there.' 'But couldn't we go straight to the place where your friend lives?' 'No, I don't know the name of the street.' 'You don't know the name of the street?' 'No, I've never noticed it.'

When I see how anxiously he is watching the meter I am sorry I insisted on taking the taxi. All the same, I should have dropped dead if I had tried to walk this distance.

'Do let me pay, because it was I who insisted.'

But he has got the money in his hand already and is counting it out.

He takes my arm and we walk along. 'It's just a minute, it's just a minute,' he keeps saying.

Walking to the music of *L'Arlésienne*, remembering the coat I wore then – a black-and-white check with big pockets. We have just passed the hotel I lived in. That was the high spot – when I had nothing to eat for three weeks, except coffee and a croissant in the morning.

I slept most of the time. Probably that was why it was so easy. If I had had to go about a lot I might have felt worse. I got so that I could sleep fifteen hours out of the twenty-four.

Twice I said I was ill, and they sent me up soup with meat in it from downstairs, and I could get an occasional bottle of wine on tick from the shop round the corner. It wasn't starvation at all when you come to think of it. Still, I'm not saying that there weren't some curious moments.

After the first week I made up my mind to kill myself – the usual whiff of chloroform. Next week, or next month, or next year I'll kill myself. But I might as well last out my month's rent, which has been paid up, and my credit for breakfasts in the morning.

'My child, don't hurry. You have eternity in front of you.' She used to say that sarcastically, Sister Marie-Augustine, because I was so slow. But the phrase stayed with me. I have eternity in front of me. Soon I'll be able to do it, but there's no hurry. Eternity is in front of me....

Usually, in the interval between my afternoon sleep and my night sleep I went for a walk, turned up the Boulevard Arago, walked to a certain spot and turned back. And one evening I was walking along with my hands in the pockets of my coat and my head down. This was the time when I got in the habit of walking with my head down. ... I was walking along in a dream, a haze, when a man came up and spoke to me.

This is unhoped-for. It's also quite unwanted. What I really want to do is to go for my usual walk, get a bottle of wine on tick and go back to the hotel to sleep. However, it has happened, and there you are. Life is curious when it is reduced to its essentials.

Well, we go into the Café Buffalo. Will I have a little apéritif? I certainly will. Two Pernods arrive.

I start thinking about food. Choucroute, for instance – you ought to be able to get choucroute garnie here. Lovely sausage, lovely potato, lovely, lovely cabbage. ... My mouth starts watering violently. I drink half the glass of Pernod in order to swallow convenablement. And then I feel like a goddess. It might have made me sick, but it has done the other thing.

The orchestra was playing *L'Arlésienne*, I remember so well. I've just got to hear that music now, any time, and I'm back in the Café Buffalo, sitting by that man. And the music going heavily. And he's talking away about a friend who is so rich that he has his photograph on the bands of his cigars. A mad conversation.

'One day,' he says, 'I too will be so rich that I shall have my photo on the bands of the cigars I offer to my friends. That is my ambition.'

Will I have another little Pernod? I certainly will have another little Pernod. (Food? I don't want any food now. I want more of this feeling – fire and wings.)

There we are, jabbering away as if we had known each other for years. He reads me a letter that he has just had from a girl.

What's the matter with it? It seems to me a letter any man ought to be proud to have. All about frissons and spasms and unquestionable réussites. (Chéri, chéri, rappelles-tu que....) A testimonial, that letter is.

But the snag is at the end, as usual. The girl wants a new pair of shoes and she is asking for three hundred francs to buy them. Chéri, you will remember the unforgettable hours we passed together and not refuse me when I tell you that my shoes are quite worn out. I am ashamed to go into the street. The valet de chambre knows that there are large holes in both my shoes. Really, I am ashamed to be so poor. I stay all the time in my room. And so, chéri, etcetera, etcetera, etcetera....

He is chewing and chewing over this letter. 'I don't believe it,' he says. 'It's all a lie, it's a snare, it's a trap. This girl, you understand, is a liar. What she wants is three hundred francs to give to her maquereau. Will I give her three hundred francs for her maquereau? No, I won't. I will not.... All the same,' he says, 'I can't bear to think of that poor little one with holes in her shoes. That can't be amusing, walking about with your feet on the ground.'

'No, it isn't amusing,' I say. 'Especially on a rainy day.'

'Well, what do you think? Do you think this letter can be genuine? What do you think?'

Every word has been chewed over by the time we have finished our second drink.

'Besides,' he says, 'even if it is genuine, I mustn't send the money at once. That would never do. If she thought she had only to ask, to have – that would never do. No, no, I must keep her waiting.'

Chew, chew, chew....

'No. I think she's lying.'

All the time he is staring at me, sizing me up. He has his hand on my knee under the table.

He is not a Parisian. He lives in Lille. He is staying at a friend's flat, he says, and it's a very nice flat. Will I come along there and have a little porto? ... Well, why not?

What does this man look like? I don't remember. I don't think I ever looked at him. I remember that he had very small hands and that he wore a ring with a blue stone in it.

We get out into the street. And, of course, vlung – first breath of fresh air and I'm so drunk I can't walk.

'Hé là,' he says. 'What's the matter? Have you been dancing too much?'

'All you young women,' he says, 'dance too much. Mad for pleasure, all the young people. ... Ah, what will happen to this after-war generation? I ask myself. What will happen? Mad for pleasure. ... But we'll take a taxi.'

We cross the road unsteadily and stand under a sickly town-tree waiting to signal a taxi. I start to giggle. He runs his hand up and down my arm.

I say: 'Do you know what's really the matter with me? I'm hungry. I've had hardly anything to eat for three weeks.'

'Comment?' he says, snatching his hand. 'What's this you're relating?'

'C'est vrai,' I say, giggling still more loudly. 'It's quite true. I've had nothing to eat for three weeks.' (Exaggerating, as usual.)

At this moment a taxi draws up. Without a word he gets into it, bangs the door and drives off, leaving me standing there on the pavement.

And did I mind? Not at all, not at all. If you think I minded, then you've never lived like that, plunged in a dream, when all the faces are masks and only the trees are alive and you can almost see the strings that are pulling the puppets. Close-up of human nature – isn't it worth something?

I expect that man thought Fate was conspiring against him – what with his girl's shoes and me wanting food. But there you are, if you're determined to get people on the cheap, you shouldn't be so surprised when they pitch you their own little story of misery sometimes.

In the middle of the night you wake up. You start to cry. What's happening to me? Oh, my life, oh, my youth. ...

There's some wine left in the bottle. You drink it. The clock ticks. Sleep. ...

People talk about the happy life, but that's the happy life when you don't care any longer if you live or die.

You only get there after a long time and many misfortunes. And do you think you are left there? Never.

As soon as you have reached this heaven of indifference, you are pulled out of it. From your heaven you have to go back to hell. When you are dead to the world, the world often rescues you, if only to make a figure of fun out of you.

Walking to the music of *L'Arlésienne*. ... I feel for the pockets of the check coat, and I am surprised when I touch the fur of the one I am wearing. ... Pull yourself together, dearie. This is late October, 1937, and that old coat had its last outing a long time ago.

We go up the stairs of a block of studios into a large, empty, cold room, with masks on the walls, two old armchairs and a straight-backed wooden chair on which is written 'merde'. The answer, the final answer, to everything?

The friend is a Jew of about forty. He has that mocking look of the Jew, the look that can be so hateful, that can be so attractive, that can be so sad.

He keeps putting bits of screwed-up newspaper into the stove.

'It won't burn. It's in a bad mood today. I'll get tea,' he says. 'The water will be boiling soon.'

'West African masks?'

'Yes, straight from the Congo. ... I made them. This one isn't bad.'

He takes it down and shows it to me. The close-set eyeholes stare into mine. I know that face very well; I've seen lots like it, complete with legs and body.

That's the way they look when they are saying: 'Why didn't you drown yourself in the Seine?' That's the way they look when they are saying: 'Qu'est-ce qu'elle fout ici, la vieille?' That's the way they look when they are saying: 'What's this story?' Peering at you. Who are you, anyway? Who's your father and have you got any money, and if not, why not? Are you one of us? Will you think what you're told to think and say what you ought to say? Are you red, white or blue – jelly, suet pudding or ersatz caviare?

Serge puts some béguine music, Martinique music, on an old gramophone in the corner and asks whether I'd like to dance.

'No, I'd rather watch you.'

He holds the mask over his face and dances. 'To make you laugh,' he says. He dances very well. His thin, nervous body looks strange, surmounted by the hideous mask. Delmar, very serious and correct, claps his hands in time to the music.

(*Have you been dancing too much?*) 'Don't stop.'

(*Mad for pleasure, all the young people.*) 'Please don't stop.'

The gramophone is grinding out 'Maladie d'amour, maladie de la jeunesse....'

I am lying in a hammock looking up into the branches of a tree. The sound of the sea advances and retreats as if a door were being opened and shut. All day there has been a fierce wind blowing, but at sunset it drops. The hills look like clouds and the clouds like fantastic hills.

> Pain of love,
> Pain of youth,
> Walk away from me,
> Keep away from me,
> Don't want to see you
> No more, no more....

Then we talk about negro music and about various boîtes in Montparnasse. The Highball? No, the Highball isn't nice any more. It's a dirty place now. Oh, is it? Yes, it is. Nobody goes there now. But the Cuban Cabin in Montmartre, that's quite good. You might like that. They play very well there. It's gay.

I am talking away, quite calmly and sedately, when

there it is again – tears in my eyes, tears rolling down my face. (Saved, rescued, but not quite so good as new. . . .)

'I'm so sorry. I'm such a fool. I don't know what's the matter with me.'

'Oh, madame, oh, madame,' Delmar says, 'why do you cry?'

'I'm such a fool. Please don't take any notice of me. Just don't take any notice and I'll be all right.'

'But cry,' le peintre says. 'Cry if you want to. Why shouldn't you cry? You're with friends.'

'If I could have a drink. . . .'

'A drink. I have some porto somewhere.'

He bustles around. He produces three very small cups – the things you drink saké from.

'Japanese,' I say, intelligently.

He doesn't answer. He is searching for the bottle of port.

He pours out what is left of it. It just fills one saké cup. That, a drink!

I have an irresistible longing for a long, strong drink to make me forget that once again I have given damnable human beings the right to pity me and laugh at me.

I say in a loud, aggressive voice: 'Go out and get a bottle of brandy,' take money out of my bag and offer it to him.

This is where he starts getting hold of me, Serge. He doesn't accept the money or refuse it – he ignores it. He blots out what I have said and the way I said it. He ignores it as if it had never been, and I know that, for him, it has never been. He is thinking of something else.

'Don't drink just now,' he says. 'Later, I'll get some, if you like. I'll make you some tea now.'

He comes back with the tea and puts lemon into it. It tastes good to me.

'I often want to cry. That is the only advantage women have over men – at least they can cry.'

We seriously discuss the subject of weeping.

Delmar doesn't cry easily, he says. No, not so easily as all that. Le peintre, it seems, cries about Van Gogh. He speechifies about 'the terrible effort, the sustained effort – something beyond the human brain, what he did.' Etcetera, etcetera. ...

When he gives me a cigarette his hand is shaking. He isn't lying. I think he has really cried over Van Gogh.

We drink more tea. The stove has quite gone out and it is very cold, but they don't seem to notice it. I am glad of my coat. I think I ought to ask to see his pictures, but he is in a flow of talk which I can't interrupt. He is relating an experience he had in London.

'Oh, you've lived in London?'

'Yes, I was there for a time, but I didn't stay long – no. But I got a fine suit,' he says. 'I looked quite an Englishman from the neck down. I was very proud. ... I had a room near Notting Hill Gate. Do you know it?'

'Oh yes, I know it.'

'A very comfortable room. But one night this happened. Talking about weeping – I still think of it. ... I was sitting by the fire, when I heard a noise as if someone had fallen down outside. I opened the door and there was a woman lying full-length in the passage, crying. I said to her: "What's the matter?" She only went on crying. "Well," I thought, "it's nothing to do with me." I shut the door firmly. But still I could hear her. I opened the door again and I asked her: "What is it? Can I do anything for you?" She said: "I want a drink." '

'Exactly like me,' I say. 'I cried, and I asked for a drink.' He certainly likes speechifying, this peintre. Is he getting at me?

'No, no,' he says. 'Not like you at all.'

He goes on: 'I said to her "Come in if you wish. I have some whisky." She wasn't a white woman. She was half-negro – a mulatto. She had been crying so much that it was impossible to tell whether she was pretty or ugly or young or old. She was drunk too, but that wasn't why she was crying. She was crying because she was at the end of everything. There was that sound in her sobbing which is quite unmistakable – like certain music. ... I put my arm round her, but it wasn't like putting your arm round a woman. She was like something that has turned into stone. She asked again for whisky. I gave it to her, and she started a long story, speaking sometimes in French, sometimes in English, when of course I couldn't understand her very well. She came from Martinique, she said, and she had met this monsieur in Paris, the monsieur she was with on the top floor. Everybody in the house knew she wasn't married to him, but it was even worse that she wasn't white. She said that every time they looked at her she could see how they hated her, and the people in the streets looked at her in the same way. At first she didn't mind – she thought it comical. But now she had got so that she would do anything not to see people. She told me she hadn't been out, except after dark, for two years. When she said this I had an extraordinary sensation, as if I were looking down into a pit. It was the expression in her eyes. I said: "But this monsieur you are living with, what about him?" "Oh, he is very Angliche, he says I imagine everything." I asked if he didn't find it strange that she never went out. But she said No, he thought it quite natural. She talked for a long time about this monsieur. It seemed that she stayed with him because she didn't know where else to go, and he stayed with her because he liked the way she cooked. All this sounds a little ridiculous, but if you had seen this woman you'd understand why it is I have never been able to forget her. I said to her: "Don't let yourself get hysterical, because if you do that it's the end." But it was difficult to speak to her reasonably, because I had all the time this feeling that I was talking to something that was no longer quite human, no longer quite alive.'

'It's a very sad story,' I say. 'I'm sure you were kind to her.'

'But that's just it. I wasn't. She told me that that afternoon she'd felt better and wanted to go out for a walk. "Even though it wasn't quite dark," she said. On the way out she had met the little girl of one of the other tenants. This house was one of those that are let off in floors. There were several families living in it. She said to the little girl: "Good afternoon. ..." It was a long story, and of course, as I said, I couldn't understand everything she said to me. But it seemed that the child had told her that she was a dirty woman, that she smelt bad, that she hadn't any right in the house. "I hate you and I wish you were dead," the child said. And after that she had drunk a whole bottle of whisky and there she was, outside my door. Well, what can you say to a story like that? I knew all the time that what she wanted was that I should make love to her and that it was the only thing that would do her any good. But alas, I couldn't. I just gave her what whisky I had and she went off, hardly able to walk. ... There were two other women in the house. There was one with a shut, thin mouth and a fat one with a bordel laugh. I must say I never heard them speaking to the Martiniquaise, but they had cruel eyes, both of them. ... I didn't much like the way they looked at me, either. ... But perhaps all women have cruel eyes. What do you think?'

I say: 'I think most human beings have cruel eyes.' That rosy, wooden, innocent cruelty. I know.

'When I passed her on the stairs next day I said good morning, but she didn't answer me. ... Once I saw the child putting her tongue out at the poor creature. Only seven or eight, and yet she knew so exactly how to be cruel and who it was safe to be cruel to. One must admire Nature. ... I got an astonishing hatred of the house after that. Every time I went in it was as if I were walking into a wall – one of those walls where people are built in, still alive. I've never forgotten this. Seriously, all the time I was in London, I felt as if I were being suffocated, as if a large derrière was sitting on me.'

'Well, some people feel that way and other people, of course, don't. It all depends.'

'But it's six o'clock. Would you mind if I leave you here with my friend, and he will show you everything. Please stay. I'll be back in an hour. But I must go now. I promised, and I shall be already half an hour late. Vous êtes chez vous.'

A dialogue with Delmar as to the best way to get to this place, which seems to be in the Rue du Bac. He turns at the door and, with the mocking expression very apparent, says something in Russian. At least, I suppose it's Russian.

Delmar puts on a feeble light in the middle of the room, then comes up to me and, in a hesitating way, takes my hand and kisses it. Then he kisses my cheek.

'When you cried I was so sad.'

I kiss him. Two loud, meaningless kisses, like a French general when he gives a decoration. Nice boy....

'What did he say before he went out?'

'He said that if you didn't want to buy a picture you needn't buy one. Nobody expects you to.'

'Oh, but I do. I absolutely want one.'

'Wait, I know how we can arrange it, so that you can really see the pictures.'

There are a lot of empty frames stacked up against the wall. Delmar arranges them round the room and puts the canvases one by one into them. The canvases resist. They curl up; they don't want to go into frames. He pushes and prods them so that they go in and stay in, in some sort of fashion.

'Ought we to do this? What will he say when he comes back?'

'Oh, it doesn't matter. It's all right. I want you to be able to see them.'

When he has finished pictures are propped up on the floor round three sides of the room.

'Now you can see them,' he says.

'Yes, now I can see them.'

I am surrounded by the pictures. It is astonishing how vivid they are in this dim light. ... Now the room expands and the iron band round my heart loosens. The miracle has happened. I am happy.

Looking at the pictures, I go off into a vague dream. Pehaps one day I'll live again round the corner in a room as empty as this. Nothing in it but a bed and a looking-glass. Getting the stove lit at about two in the afternoon – the cold and the stove fighting each other. Lying near the stove in complete peace, having some bread with pâté spread on it, and then having a drink and lying all the afternoon in that empty room – nothing in it but the bed, the stove and the looking-glass and outside Paris. And the dreams that you have, alone in an empty room, waiting for the door that will open, the thing that is bound to happen....

It is after seven when Serge comes back. He rushes in, panting: 'I'm sorry I'm late.' He talks to Delmar in Russian. Is he saying: 'Well, was she any good?' or is he saying: 'Will she buy a picture and is she going to pay up?' The last, I think – the tone was businesslike.

'I want very much to buy one of your pictures – this one.'

It is an old Jew with a red nose, playing the banjo.

'The price of that is six hundred francs,' he says. 'If you think it's too much we'll arrange some other price.'

All his charm and ease of manner have gone. He looks anxious and surly. I say awkwardly: 'I don't think it at all too much. But I haven't got the money....'

Before I can get any further he bursts into a shout of laughter. 'What did I tell you?' he says to Delmar.

'But have it, take it, all the same. I like you. I'll give it you as a present.'

'No, no. All I meant was that I can't pay you now.'

'Oh, that's all right. You can send me the money from

London. I'll tell you what you can do for me – you can find some other idiots who'll buy my pictures.'

When he says this, he smiles at me so gently, so disarmingly. The touch of the human hand. ... I'd forgotten what it was like, the touch of the human hand.

'I'm serious. I mean that. Take the picture and send me the money when you can.'

'I can let you have it tonight.'

We argue for some time as to where we shall meet.

'I can't stand Montparnasse now,' he says. 'Those faces, those gueules! They make me sick. Somewhere in the Quartier Latin.'

We decide on the Capoulade at half-past ten. He rolls up the picture in tissue-paper, ties it round with a bit of string and I take it under my arm. Then he gives my hand a long, hard shake and says 'Amis'.

When he shakes my hand like that and says 'Amis' I feel very happy....

We get out into the courtyard, Delmar and I. It is a very cold, clear night. The outer door is shut. Business with the concierge.

Now I am not thinking of the past at all. I am well in the present.

'Capoulade – half-past ten....'

The pictures walk along with me. The misshapen dwarfs juggle with huge coloured balloons, the four-breasted woman is exhibited, the old prostitute waits hopelessly outside the urinoir, the young one under the bec de gaz....

At ten-twenty-five – still fairly exalted – I am in the Capoulade. I wait for a quarter of an hour, twenty minutes. Nobody turns up. ... Bon, bien, that's what you get for being exalted, my girl. But the protective armour is functioning all right – I don't mind at all.

I am just worrying about the way I am going to give this man his money. I can't write, because I don't remember the number of the house. Shall I push it under the door of his studio and trust to luck?

As I am thinking this Delmar comes in. Correct, gloves in his left hand.

'Oh, I'm so sorry, so sorry. I waited at the studio for le peintre for half an hour and he never turned up. I didn't know what to do. I thought it was better to come here. I've been so worried about it.'

'That's all right. It doesn't matter at all.'

I give him the envelope with the money.

Is there a closing of the eyes, a slightly relieved expression on his face? Yes, I think so. And why not? Have a heart. Why not?

However, he does seem annoyed – so far as he can be annoyed, which isn't very far. Here is someone who firmly believes in his own creed: 'I didn't ask to be born, I didn't ask to be put into the world, I didn't make myself, I didn't make the world as it is, I am a guiltless one. So I have the right,' etcetera, etcetera, etcetera. ...

'Le peintre!' he says. 'Il est fou, le peintre. ... Did you like him?'

'Yes, I liked him very much.'

He lays his gloves carefully down on the table.

'Will you have a coffee, madame?'

'No, I'll have a brandy, please.'

He looks anxious, orders the brandy and a coffee for himself. God, this is awful!

'Le peintre,' he says, 'he's mad. I don't know why he has been so impolite, but it's just what he would do. Because he's mad. You know, two years ago, this man, he was living. ... Terrible. ... La crasse, madame. ... I said to him: "You can't go on living like this." "Je m'en fous," he said. ... However, I talked to him and in the end he managed to get the money to give his exhibition. And his pictures were bought. Yes, they were bought. ...

Eighteen thousand francs. C'est inouï, une somme pareille. . . . And then he did move. He went to this beautiful, respectable room where you saw him. . . . All the same he is mad.'

He goes on talking about le peintre. I gather that he is impressed but jealous. He can't see the attraction. Why, why?

'So you liked him?'

'Yes, I did. Very much.'

'Ah,' he says, gloomily, 'voilà. All the same, I've had enough of these people of the extreme Left. They have bad manners. Moi, je suis monarchiste. . . . And, mind you, when he says he is of the extreme Left, it's all nonsense. He doesn't really care.'

'Of course he doesn't.'

'Yes, yes. . . . Moi, je suis monarchiste. A queen, for instance, a princess – that must be something.'

If he feels like that, what's the use of arguing with him? . . . I agree with everything. A queen, a princess – that's something.

When he asks if I can meet him again: 'Well, I'll try,' I say. 'But I'm very much occupied.'

I can't stand this business of not being able to have what I want to drink, because he won't allow me to pay and certainly doesn't want to pay himself. It's too wearing.

'I'm leaving Paris next week. Sooner than I thought.'

Will I let him know when I am going, so that he can come to the Gare du Nord to see me off?

'Yes, please do. It would be so nice if you would. It's sad to go away from a place with nobody to tell you good-bye.'

When I am back in my room I start worrying about him and the money he has spent on me. And then I think: 'I bet he'll get his percentage on that six hundred francs. Or perhaps he won't hand the money over at all.'

This idea makes me laugh all the time I am undressing.

•

Wandering about the narrow streets near the Panthéon. It starts to rain.

I go into a tabac. The woman at the bar gives me one of those looks: What do you want here, you? We don't cater for tourists here, not our clientèle. ... Well, dear madame, to tell you the truth, what I want here is a drink – I rather think two, perhaps three.

It is cold and dark outside, and everything has gone out of me except misery.

'A Pernod,' I say to the waiter.

He looks at me in a sly, amused way when he brings it.

God, it's funny, being a woman! And the other one – the one behind the bar – is she going to giggle or to say something about me in a voice loud enough for me to hear? That's the way she's feeling.

No, she says nothing. ... But she says it all.

Well, that's O.K., chère madame, and very nicely done too. You've said nothing but you've said it all. Never mind, here I am and here I'm going to stay.

Behind my table there is a door. Toilette – they needn't have said so. And then another, smaller door. Service. I hear noises of washing-up going on behind this door.

After a while a girl comes out, with a tray piled with clean glasses. She leaves the door open. Inside, a sink, a tap and more dirty glasses and plates, waiting to be washed. There is just room for the girl to stand. An unbelievable smell comes from the sink.

She passes me without looking at me. Bare, sturdy legs, felt slippers, a black dress, a filthy apron, thick, curly, untidy hair. I know her. This is the girl who does all the dirty work and gets paid very little for it. Salut!

She goes into the room behind the bar, puts the glasses down, walks back to the cupboard and shuts herself in again. How does she manage not to knock her elbows every time she moves? How can she stay in that coffin for five minutes without fainting? ... Sorry for her? Why should I be sorry for her? Hasn't she got sturdy legs and curly hair? And don't her strong hands sing the Marseillaise? And when the revolution comes, won't those be the hands to be kissed? Well, so Monsieur Rimbaud says, doesn't he? I hope he's right. I wonder, though, I wonder, I wonder. ...

I call the waiter, to pay. I give him a large tip. He looks at it, says 'Merci', and then 'Merci beaucoup'. I ask him to tell me the way to the nearest cinema. This, of course, arises from a cringing desire to explain my presence in the place. I only came in here to inquire the way to the nearest cinema. I am a respectable woman, une femme convenable, on her way to the nearest cinema. Faites comme les autres – that's been my motto all my life. Faites comme les autres, damn you.

And a lot he cares – I could have spared myself the trouble. But this is my attitude to life. Please, please, monsieur et madame, mister, missis and miss, I am trying so hard to be like you. I know I don't succeed, but look how hard I try. Three hours to choose a hat; every morning an hour and a half trying to make myself look like everybody else. Every word I say has chains round its ankles; every thought I think is weighted with heavy weights. Since I was born, hasn't every word I've said, every thought I've thought, everything I've done, been tied up, weighted, chained? And, mind you, I know that with all this I don't succeed. Or I succeed in flashes only too damned well. ... But think how hard I try and how seldom I dare. Think – and have a bit of pity. That is, if you ever think, you apes, which I doubt.

Now the waiter has finished telling me how to get to the nearest cinema.

'Another Pernod,' I say.

He brings it. He fills my glass almost to the brim, perhaps in anticipation of another tip, perhaps because he wants to see me drunk as soon as possible, or perhaps because the bottle slipped.

The girl comes out with the last lot of glasses. I'm

glad. It has just occurred to me that if I weren't here the door of her coffin might be kept open. *Might* be. Not that I would have gone away if it had occurred to me before. Why should I? The hands that sing the Marseillaise, the world that could be so different – what's all that to me? What can I do about it? Nothing. I don't deceive myself.

That's settled. I can start on the second Pernod.

Now the feeling of the room is different. They all know what I am. I'm a woman come in here to get drunk. That happens sometimes. They have a drink, these women, and then they have another and then they start crying silently. And then they go into the lavabo and then they come out – powdered, but with hollow eyes – and, head down, slink into the street.

'Poor woman, she has tears in her eyes.'

'What do you expect? Elle a bu.'

That's it, chère madame, I'm drunk. I have drunk. There's nothing to be done about it now. I have drunk. But otherwise quiet, fearful, tamed, prepared to give big tips. (I'll give a big tip if you'll leave me alone.) Bon, bien, bien, bon. ...

Sometimes somebody comes in for stamps, or a man for a drink. Then you can see outside into the street. And the street walks in. It is one of those streets – dark, powerful, magical. ...

'Oh, there you are,' it says, walking in at the door, 'there you are. Where have you been all this long time?'

Nobody else knows me but the street knows me.

'And there you are,' I say, finishing my Pernod and rather drunk. 'Salut, salut!'

(But sometimes it was sunny. ... Walking along in the sun in a gay dress, striped red and blue. ... I won't walk along that street again.)

The Cinéma Danton. Watching a good young man trying to rescue his employer from a mercenary mistress. The employer is a gay, bad old boy who manufactures toilet articles. The good young man has the awkwardness, the smugness, the shyness, the pathos of good young men. He interrupts intimate conversations, knocking loudly, bringing in letters and parcels, etcetera, etcetera. At last the lady, annoyed, gets up and sweeps away. She turns at the door to say: 'Alors, bien, je te laisse à tes suppositoires.' Everybody laughs loudly at this, and so do I. She said that well.

The film goes on and on. After many vicissitudes, the good young man is triumphant. He has permission to propose to his employer's daughter. He is waiting on the bank of a large pond, with a ring that he is going to offer her ready in his waistcoat pocket. He takes it out to make sure that he has it. Mad with happiness, he strides up and down the shores of the pond, gesticulating. He makes too wild a gesture. The ring flies from his hand into the middle of the pond. He takes off his trousers; he wades out. He has to get the ring back; he must get it back.

Exactly the sort of thing that happens to me. I laugh till the tears come into my eyes. However, the film shows no signs of stopping, so I get up and go out.

Another Pernod in the bar next door to the cinema. I sit at a corner table and sip it respectably, with lowered eyes. Je suis une femme convenable, just come out of the nearest cinema. ... Now I really am O.K., chère madame. If I have a bottle of Bordeaux at dinner I'll be almost as drunk as I'd hoped to be.

There is a letter from le peintre at the hotel. He says he is very sorry he didn't turn up the other evening – il faut m'excuser. He says Delmar has handed over the six hundred francs, and he thanks me. He says that if I don't like the bonhomme, if I find him too sad, he will change him for one of the landscapes or for anything else I want and that he will try to get to the Gare du Nord to say au revoir to me (I bet he won't), and he is my friend, Serge Rubin.

Well, I'll have a whisky on that.

I unroll the picture and the man standing in the gutter, playing his banjo, stares at me. He is gentle, humble, resigned, mocking, a little mad. He stares at me. He is double-headed, doubled-faced. He is singing 'It has been', singing 'It will be'. Double-headed and with four arms. ... I stare back at him and think about being hungry, being cold, being hurt, being ridiculed, as if it were in another life than this.

This damned room – it's saturated with the past. ... It's all the rooms I've ever slept in, all the streets I've ever walked in. Now the whole thing moves in an ordered, undulating procession past my eyes. Rooms, streets, streets, rooms. ...

Part Three

... The room at the Steens'.

It was crowded with red plush furniture, the wood shining brightly. There were several vases of tulips and two cages with canaries, and there were two clocks, each trying to tick louder than the other. The windows were nearly always shut, but the room wasn't musty. When the door into the shop was open you could smell drugs and eau-de-Cologne. On a table at the back there was a big pot of tea over a spirit-lamp. The little blue light made it look like an altar.

In that room you couldn't think, you couldn't make plans. Just the way the clocks ticked, and outside the clean, narrow streets, and the others talking Dutch and I listening, not understanding. It was like being a child again, listening and thinking of something else and hearing the voices – endless, inevitable and restful. Like Sunday afternoon.

Well, London. ... It has a fine sound, but what was London to me? It was a little room, smelling stuffy, with my stockings hanging to dry in front of a gas-fire. Nothing in that room was ever clean; nothing was ever dirty, either. Things were always half-and-half. They changed one sheet at a time, so that the bed was never quite clean and never quite dirty.

Thinking: 'I've got away from all that, anyhow. Not to go back, not to go back....'

I liked Tonny; she was gentle. But I hated Hans Steen. He had a blustering look. He didn't bluster, he was very polite. But his pale blue eyes had that look, and his hands.

Narrow streets, with the people walking up one way and down another. So tidily. In the park, the Haagsche Bosch, the trees upside-down in the ice green water.

We go every day to the Centraal for an apéritif. We eat at a little place where the violinist plays sentimental tunes very well. ('Will you play *Le Binyou* for madame? ...')

I haven't any money. He hasn't any either. We both thought the other had money. But people are doing crazy things all over the place. The war is over. No more war – never, never, never. Après la guerre, there'll be a good time everywhere. ... And not to go back to London. It isn't so fine, what I have to go back to in London.

But no money? Nix? ... And the letter in my handbag: 'I think you must be mad. If you insist on doing this. ...'

A tall vase of sprawling tulips on the table. How they give themselves! 'Perhaps it's because they know they have nothing to give,' Enno says.

Talking about Paris, where he has lived since he was eighteen. He was a chansonnier, it seems, before he became a journalist. He enlisted during the first week of the war. From 1917 onwards a gap. He seemed very prosperous when I met him in London, but now no money – nix. What happened? He doesn't tell me.

But when we get to Paris the good life will start again. Besides, we have money. Between us we have fifteen pounds.

All the same, I never thought we should really get married. One day I'll make a plan, I'll know what to do. ...

Then I wake up and it's my wedding-day, cold and rainy. I put on the grey suit that a tailor in Delft has made for me on tick. I don't like it much. Enno comes in with a bunch of lilies-of-the-valley, pins it in my coat and kisses me. We get a taxi and drive through the rain to the town-hall and we are married with a lot of other couples, all standing round in a circle. We come out of the town-hall and have one drink with Tonny and Hans. Then they go home to look after the shop. We go on to another place. Nobody else is there – it's too early. We have two glasses of port and then another two.

'How idiotic all that business was!' Enno says.

We have more port. It's the first time that day that I have felt warm or happy.

I say: 'You won't ever leave me, will you?'

'Allons, allons, a little gaiety,' Enno says.

He has a friend called Dickson, a Frenchman, who sings at the Scala. He calls himself Dickson because English singers are popular at the moment. We go to his flat that afternoon and drink champagne. Everybody gets very gay. Louis and Louise, tango dancers, also at the cabaret, do their show for us. Dickson sings *In These Hard Times*:

> That funny kind of dress you wear
> Leaves all your back and your shoulders bare,
> But you're lucky to be dressed up to there
> In these hard times.

Enno sings:

> Quand on n'a pas de chaussures
> On fait comme les rentiers,
> On prend une voiture,
> On ne vous voit pas les pieds!
>
> Parlons donc de chaussettes:
> Faut pas les nettoyer,
> On les retourne, c'est pas bête,
> Puis on les change de pied!

I sing: 'For tonight, for tonight, Let me dream out my dream of delight, Tra-la-la. ... And purchase from sorrow a moment's respite, Tra-la-la....'

Mrs Dickson reads aloud excitedly from a theatrical

paper. Two girls they know are mixed up in a murder case. She reads about Riri and Cricri, rolling her 'r's'. Rrrirrri, Crrricri. ...

I am a bit drunk when we take the train to Amsterdam.

•

... *The room in the hotel in Amsterdam that night.*

It was very clean, with a rose-patterned wallpaper.

'Now, you mustn't worry about money,' Enno says. 'Money's a stupid thing to worry about. You let me do. I can always get some. When we get to Paris it'll be all right.'

(*When – we – get – to – Paris. ...*)

There's another bottle of champagne on the table by the bed.

'Love,' Enno says, 'you mustn't talk about love. Don't talk. ...'

You mustn't talk, you mustn't think, you must stop thinking. Of course, it is like that. You must let go of everything else, stop thinking. ...

Next morning we eat an enormous breakfast of sausages, cold meat, cheese and milk. We walk about Amsterdam. We look at pictures in the Rijksmuseum. 'Would you like to see your double?' Enno says.

I am tuned up to top pitch. Everything is smooth, soft and tender. Making love. The colours of the pictures. The sunsets. Tender, north colours when the sun sets – pink, mauve, green and blue. And the wind very fresh and cold and the lights in the canals like gold caterpillars and the seagulls swooping over the water. Tuned up to top pitch. Everything tender and melancholy – as life is sometimes, just for one moment. ... And when we get to Paris; *when – we – get – to – Paris. ...*

'I want very much to go back to Paris,' Enno would say. 'It has no reason, no sense. But all the same I want to go back there. Certain houses, certain streets. ... No sense, no reason. Just this nostalgia. ... And, mind you, some of my songs have made money....'

Suddenly I am in a fever of anxiety to get there. Let's be on our way, let's be on our way. ... Why shouldn't we get as far as Brussels? All right, we'll get as far as Brussels; might be something doing in Brussels.

But the fifteen pounds have gone. We raise every penny we can. We sell most of our clothes.

My beautiful life in front of me, opening out like a fan in my hand....

*

What happened then? ... Well, what happens?

The room in the Brussels hotel – very hot. The bell of the cinema next door ringing. A long, narrow room with a long narrow window and the bell of the cinema next door, sharp and meaningless.

Things haven't gone. Enno saying: 'We've only got thirty francs left.' (My Lord, is that all?) 'Yes, only thirty francs. We'll have to do something about it tomorrow.'

The bell of the cinema kept on ringing and every time it rang I could feel him start.

When he went out next morning he said: 'I think I'll be able to raise some money. Wait in here for me.'

'Will you be a long time?'

'No.... Anyhow, don't go out.'

Sitting on the bed, waiting. Walking up and down the room, waiting. I can't stand it, this waiting.

Then, as if somebody had spoken it aloud in my head – Mr Lawson. Of course, Mr Lawson....

I hadn't remembered how glassy his eyes were, Mr Lawson's.

'Yes?' he says. 'You asked to see me?' Raising his eyebrows a little, he says: 'Ye-es?'

He doesn't recognize me. I must look rather awful.

I say: 'I'm afraid you don't remember me. I was staying

in those rooms in the Temple that you came to look over, and you took me to dinner. We had oysters and we talked about Ireland. Don't you remember? Then we were on the boat going over to Holland and you gave me your address in Brussels. You said if I got here, would I look you up? Don't you remember?'

'Of course. Little Miss –'

'Not little,' I say, 'not little.' Because I can't have a man like that calling me little.

I talk away, saying, as if it were a joke: 'We're not exactly stranded. We shall be quite all right as soon as we get to Paris. In fact, we shall be quite all right in a day or two. Only, stupidly, just for the moment, we're a bit stranded.'

Mr Lawson talks back and in the end he gives me a hundred francs. 'If this is any good to you. And now, I'm very sorry, but I've got to rush.'

I am standing there with the note in my hand, when he comes up to me and kisses me. I am hating him more than I have ever hated anyone in my life, yet I feel my mouth go soft under his, and my arms go limp. 'Good-bye,' he says in imitation American, and grins.

'Did you have any luck?'

'Not much,' Enno says.

I say: 'I've managed to borrow a hundred francs.'

'Who did you borrow it from?'

'Well, it's a woman I used to know very well in London. I knew she lived here and I found her address in the directory. She knew Miss Cavell. Yes, a friend of Miss Cavell's. She lives in the Avenue Louise, and I went and saw her.

'She's not exactly a friend,' I say. 'As a matter of fact, she was horribly rude, the old bitch. She as good as told me she wouldn't see me if ever I went there again. Mademoiselle regrette, mais mademoiselle ne reçoit pas aujourd'hui....'

'Avenue Louise? What number Avenue Louise?'

'Oh, shut up about it.' I lie down on the bed and begin to cry.

'Don't cry. If you cry I shall go mad.'

'Shut up, then, and don't talk about the damned hundred francs.' (With a hundred francs they buy the unlimited right to scorn you. It's cheap.)

'What are you crying about?' he says.

'It's my dress. I feel so awful. I feel so dirty. I want to have a bath. I want another dress. I want clean underclothes. I feel so awful. I feel so dirty.'

'I'll get you another dress as soon as we get to Paris. I know somewhere where we can get credit.... You'll see, when we get to Paris it'll be all right.'

He goes out to buy something to eat. I lie there and I am happy, forgetting everything, happy and cool, not caring if I live or die. I think of the way Mr Lawson looked at me when I first went in – his long, narrow, surprised face. I laugh and I can't stop laughing.

•

The lavatory at the station – that was the next time I cried. I had just been sick. I was so afraid I might be going to have a baby....

Although I have been so sick, I don't feel any better. I lean up against the wall, icy cold and sweating. Someone tries the door, and I pull myself together, stop crying and powder my face.

We are going to Calais. Enno has made pals with a waiter who lives there and who has promised to lend us some money.

He is very good at salad-dressing, this waiter. We eat with him and his wife next day. There he is, with his fat back and thick neck, mixing the dressing. He uses sugar in the German way. His wife watches him, looking spiteful and frightened. She is thin and ugly and not young.

The waiter mixes the dressing for the salad very slowly at the sideboard. I can see myself in the mirror. I look thin – too thin – and dirty and haggard, with that expression that you get in your eyes when you are very tired and everything is like a dream and you are starting to know what things are like underneath what people say they are.

I hadn't bargained for this. I didn't think it would be like this – shabby clothes, worn-out shoes, circles under your eyes, your hair getting straight and lanky, the way people look at you. ... I didn't think it would be like this.

Walking about the streets of Calais with the waiter's wife. We went to see that statue by Rodin. All the time she was complaining in a thin voice that he never let her have any money for clothes, and that it was her money after all; he hadn't a sou when she married him.

She didn't seem at all curious about us, or to want to know where he picked us up. She just went on and on about his unkindness and the clothes she wanted.

It was a grey day. It was like walking in London, like walking in a dream. My God, how awful I looked in that mirror! If I'm going to look like that, there's not a hope. Fancy having to go to Paris looking like that....

When we got back we drank absinthe. The waiter prepared it for us elaborately. It took a long time. I didn't like the taste, but I was cold and it warmed me. We sat there sipping and Enno and the waiter talked in a corner. The wife didn't say anything and after a while I didn't either. But the absinthe made me feel quarrelsome and I began to wish I could shout 'Shut up' at them and to dislike the waiter because I knew he wasn't thinking much of my looks. ('She's not much. I thought she was better-looking than that the first time I saw her.')

I stopped listening to them, but when the absinthe went really to my head I thought I was shouting to them to shut up. I even heard my voice saying: 'Shut up; I hate you.' But really I didn't say anything and when Enno looked at me I smiled.

Well, Gustave – the waiter – lent us the money he had promised and we left Calais.

Enno had taken a dislike to Gustave's wife. 'That to call itself a woman!' he said.

'But it was her money,' I said.

'Oh well,' Enno said, 'he makes very good use of it, doesn't he? He makes much better use of it than she would.'

It was a slow train and we were tightly packed in the compartment. Lying in the luggage-rack, trying to sleep, propped up by Enno's stick, and the wheels of the train saying: 'Paris, Paris, Paris, Paris....'

*

A girl came into the café and sat down at the next table. She was wearing a grey suit, the skirt short and tight and the blouse very fresh and clean. And a cocky black hat like a Scots soldier's glengarry. Her handbag was lying on the table near her – patent leather to match her shoes. (Handbag.... What a lot of things I've got to get! Would a suit like that be a good thing to get? No, I think I had better get....) And she walked so straight and quick on her high-heeled shoes. Tap, tap, tap, her heels....

'I'll take you somewhere to wait,' Enno said. 'I must see one or two people.'

Drinking coffee very early in the morning, everything like a dream. I was so tired.

We got out of the Métro into the Boulevard Montparnasse.

'In here,' Enno said. He took me by the arm.

The Rotonde was full of men reading newspapers on long sticks. Shabby men, not sneering, not taking any notice. Pictures on the walls.

The hands of the clock moving quickly. One hour, two hours, three hours. . . .

How long will they let me sit here? Not a drop of coffee left. The last drop was very cold and very bitter – very cold and bitter, the last drop. I have five francs, but I daren't order another coffee. I mustn't spend it on that.

The colours of the pictures melting into each other, my head back against the bench. If I go to sleep they'll certainly turn me out. Perhaps they won't, but better not risk it.

Three hours and a half. . . .

As soon as I see him I know from his face that he's got some money. A tall man is with him, a man with a gentle face and long, thin hands.

We go next door to a place called La Napolitaine and eat ravioli. Warming me. Eat slowly, make it last a long time.

I've never been so happy in my life. I'm alive, eating ravioli and drinking wine. I've escaped. A door has opened and let me out into the sun. What more do I want? Anything might happen.

'I've got a room,' Enno says. 'Rue Lamartine.'

'I had a chase,' he says. 'Paulette wasn't in. I left a note. I ran into Alfred just outside her apartment.'

Alfred smiles, bows, twists his hands nervously and departs.

'He's nice,' I say.

'Yes, he's a nice boy. He's a Turk.'

'Oh, I thought he was French.'

'No, he's a Turk.'

How much money has he got? No, don't ask. I don't want to know. Tell me later on, tell me tomorrow. Let me be happy just for now. . . .

An old man comes up, selling red roses. Enno buys some. He must have enough money for a bit.

The old boy shuffles off. Then he turns round, comes

back and puts two extra roses on the table near my plate. 'Vous permettez, monsieur?' he says to Enno, bowing like a prince.

Paris. . . . I am in Paris. . . .

•

The room we got in the hotel in the Rue Lamartine looked all right. It was on the fourth floor, the top floor. There was a big bed, covered with a red eiderdown, and outside a little balcony. You could stand and lean your arms on the cool iron and look down at the street.

We took it and paid a month's rent in advance – and that night we woke up scratching, and the wall was covered with bugs, crawling slowly.

I didn't mind the bugs much. I didn't mind anything then. . . .

'Impossible, monsieur. Mais qu'est-ce que vous me dites là? Ce n'est pas possible. Voyons. . . .' Etcetera, etcetera.

She didn't want to give the money back, and after a while it was arranged that she should have the place fumigated and give us another room while it was being done. I was glad we didn't have to leave.

I am lying on a long chair in the middle of the room, which still smells of sulphur. I have opened the door and stuck a piece of paper in it so that it shall stay open. I have shut the shutters to keep the sun out. The room is dim and the ceiling seems to be pressing on my head. I have been going through the advertisements in the *Figaro*, marking those of people who want English lessons.

Enno sits by the table, smoking his pipe. Monsieur Alfred on the bed. I watch the beads of sweat trickling down his face from his temples to his chin. I have never seen anybody sweat like that – it's extraordinary. Every now and again he blows through closed lips, takes out his handkerchief and wipes his face. Then, in a minute, it is wet and shining again.

I like Alfred. Once he said to me: 'It's very warm today. I'll make you feel cool and happy.' He took my wrist and blew on it, very gently, very regularly. I tried to take it away, didn't because he had lent us five hundred francs, then I began to feel cool, peaceful.

And Alfred recites. 'Answer with a cold silence the eternal silence of the divinity,' he says. Sweating like hell.

'Do you mind if I shut the door, madame? There's a terrible draught in this room.'

'Ah, non, mon vieux, non,' Enno says. 'Leave the door open.'

'Just as you like,' says Alfred, fingering his moustache with his long, beautiful hands. He looks shy and pained. 'I thought it wasn't good for madame to sit in a draught like this.'

'I'm not in a draught,' I say. 'I'm all right.'

Alfred goes on stroking his moustache. His eyes look malicious, in the same way that a woman's eyes look suddenly malicious.

He says, looking malicious: 'I think it's a good idea, madame, this giving lessons.' Then, speaking to Enno: 'Not a bad idea, not at all a bad idea. You get two or three good bourgeois to pay up, and afterwards – ça va. Talk, say what you like, but you can't do without the bourgeoisie.'

Enno doesn't answer.

'If I were married,' Alfred says, 'I wouldn't let my wife work for another man. No, no. I should think it a terrible disgrace to let my wife work for any other man but me. I wouldn't do it. Nothing would make me do it.'

'Tu m'emmerdes!' Enno yells, jumping up, 'tu m'emmerdes, je te dis. What are you trying to say, then?'

'Bon, bon, I'm going,' Alfred says, getting up. 'I see you are in a bad temper. I'm going. You needn't shout at me.'

'Oh, don't go,' I say.

'You shut up,' Enno says.

'Madame,' says Alfred from the door, bowing.

I laugh when he bows. I keep on saying: 'Isn't this funny, isn't this funny?' I remember Alfred blowing on my wrists to cool them and I can't stop laughing. I get so tired that I put my head into my hands.

Enno says: 'I'm going out to buy something to eat.'

'Already? It's too early.'

He goes out without answering, slamming the door.

•

'You don't know how to make love,' he said. That was about a month after we got to Paris. 'You're too passive, you're lazy, you bore me. I've had enough of this. Good-bye.'

He walked out and left me alone – that night and the next day, and the next night and the next day. With twenty francs on the table. And I'm sure now that I'm going to have a baby, though I haven't said a word about it.

I have to go out to get myself something to eat. The patron knows, the patronne knows, everybody knows. ... Waking up at night, listening, waiting. ...

The third day I make up my mind that he isn't coming back. A blue day. This is the first time that I look at the patronne instead of sliding past her with my eyes down. She inquires about monsieur. Monsieur may be away for some time.

Blue sky over the streets, the houses, the bars, the cafés, the vegetable shops and the Faubourg Montmartre. ...

I buy milk, a loaf of bread, four oranges, and go back to the hotel.

Squeezing the rind of an orange and smelling the oil. A lot of oil – they must be pretty fresh. ... I think: 'What's going to happen?' After all, I don't much care what happens. And just as I am thinking this Enno walks in with a bottle of wine under his arm.

'Hello,' he says.

'I've got some money,' he says. 'My God, isn't it hot? Peel me an orange.'

'I'm very thirsty,' he says. 'Peel me an orange.'

Now is the time to say 'Peel it yourself', now is the time to say 'Go to hell', now is the time to say 'I won't be treated like this'. But much too strong – the room, the street, the thing in myself, oh, much too strong. . . . I peel the orange, put it on a plate and give it to him.

He says; 'I've got some money.'

He brings out a mille note, a second mille note. I don't ask where he has got them. Why ask? Money circulates; it circulates – and how! Why, you wouldn't believe it sometimes.

He pours me out a glass of wine. 'It's fresh. I've kept it away from the sun.'

'But your hands are so cold,' he says. 'My girl. . . .'

He draws the curtains to keep the sun out.

When he kissed my eyelids to wake me it was dark.

But it wasn't all that that mattered. It wasn't that he knew so exactly when to be cruel, so exactly how to be kind. The day I was sure I loved him was quite different.

He had gone out to buy something to eat. I was behind the curtain and I saw him in the street below, standing by a lamp-post, looking up at our window, looking for me. He seemed very thin and small and I saw the expression on his face quite plainly. Anxious, he was. . . .

The bottle of wine was under one arm, and his coat was sticking out, because the loaf of bread was hidden under it. The patronne didn't like us to eat in our room. Just once in a while she didn't mind, but when people eat in their room every night, it means they really have no money at all.

When I saw him looking up like that I knew that I loved him, and that it was for always. It was as if my heart turned over, and I knew that it was for always. It's a strange feeling – when you know quite certainly in yourself that something is for always. It's like what death must be. All the insouciance, all the gaiety is a bluff. Because I wanted to escape from London I fastened myself on him, and I am dragging him down. All the gaiety is going and now he is thin and anxious. . . .

I didn't wave to him. I stayed by the curtain and watched him, and after a while he crossed the street and went into the hotel.

'I can't sleep,' he said. 'Let me lie with my head on your silver breast.'

•

The curtains are thin, and when they are drawn the light comes through softly. There are flowers on the window-sill and I can see their shadows on the curtains. The child downstairs is screaming.

There is a wind, and the flowers on the window-sill, and their shadows on the curtains, are waving. Like swans dipping their beaks in water. Like the incalculable raising its head, uselessly and wildly, for one moment before it sinks down, beaten, into the darkness. Like skulls on long, thin necks. Plunging wildly when the wind blows, to the end of the curtain, which is their nothingness. Distorting themselves as they plunge.

The musty smell, the bugs, the loneliness, this room, which is part of the street outside – this is all I want from life.

Things are going well. We have settled down. Enno has sold two articles. He has been to see the old boy at the Lapin Agile, and now sings there every night. And there is a real job in prospect. A publicity campaign, to popularize tea in France – Timmins' Tea. He is very excited about this, and he has designed a poster, which he says will appeal to the French: 'Tea is the most economical drink in the world. It costs less than one sou a cup.' I give English lessons. Ten francs an hour. I have three pupils – a girl who works in a scent-shop, a man who advertised in the *Figaro*, and a young Russian whom Enno met at the Lapin Agile. He speaks English just as well as I do.

I have bought a Berlitz book and follow it blindly. Farcical, these lessons, except the Russian's. He is determined to get value for his ten francs, and he does.

'Would you tell me, please, if I have the "th" correctly?' The, this, that, these, those – all correct.

He brings along a collected edition of Oscar Wilde's works and says he wants to read them through. 'Will you stop me, please, if I mispronounce a word? ... I think Oscar Wilde is the greatest of English writers. Do you agree?'

'Well....'

'Ah, you do not agree.'

'But I do like him. I think he is very – sympathique.'

He makes a little speech about English hypocrisy. Preaching to the converted.

The streets, blazing hot, and eating peaches. The long, lovely, blue days that lasted for ever, that still are. ...

At the corner of the street, the chemist's shop with the advertisement of the Abbé Something's Elixir – it cures this, it cures that, it cures the sickness of pregnant women. Would it cure mine? I wonder.

My face is pretty, my stomach is huge. Last time we ate at the Algerian restaurant I had to rush away and be sick. ... People are very kind to me. They get up and give me their seats in buses. Passe, Femme sacrée. ... Not exactly like that, but still – it seemed to me that they were kind. All the same, I'm not so mad now about going out, and I spend long hours by myself.

There is a bookshop next door, which advertises second-hand English novels. The assistant is a Hindu. I want a long, calm book about people with large incomes – a book like a flat green meadow and the sheep feeding in it. But he insists upon selling me lurid stories of the white-slave traffic. 'This is a very good book, very beautiful, most true.'

But gradually I get some books that I do like. I read most of the time and I am happy.

•

In and out of the room – Lise, Paulette, Jean, Alfred the Turk. I watch them, and I never quite know them, but I love Lise.

She is a brodeuse – or she has been a brodeuse. Now she sings English songs in a cheap cabaret in the Rue Cujas – *Roses of Picardy* and *Love, Here is My Heart*. She can't speak English at all. She is twenty-two years old, three years younger than I am.

Everything about Lise surprises me – her gentleness, her extreme sentimentality, so different from what I had been led to expect in a French girl. Airs from *Manon*, pink garters with little silk roses on them, Gyraldose. ... 'Is it true that Englishwomen never use a douche? Myself, I use one twice a day. ... And all my underclothes made by hand. Yes, every stitch.'

She has black, curly hair, a very pretty face and – unfortunately – thick ankles. ... 'I love Gounod's *Ave Maria*. The music is like a prayer, don't you think? ...' She often comes in and eats with us.

One night I am in the room with Lise. We have just had a fine meal – spaghetti cooked on the flamme bleue and a bottle of Asti spumante. I am feeling rather good.

She says: 'I wish there'd be another war.'

'Oh, Lise, don't say that.'

'Yes, I do. I might have a bit of luck. I might get killed. I don't want to live any more, me.'

Then she's off. She has nobody. She doesn't think anybody likes her. The engagement in the Rue Cujas is finished. She can't get another. She will once more have to try for a job as a brodeuse. 'And the light in the work-rooms isn't so good. Sometimes your eyes hurt so much that you can hardly open them.' She is going to have to go back to live with her mother, who keeps a grocer's shop at Clamart. She is afraid of her mother. When she was a little girl her mother beat her. 'For anything, for nothing. You don't know. And all the time she says bad things to me. She likes to make me cry. She hates me, my mother. I have no one. Soon I shall have to wear spectacles. Soon I shall be old.'

'My God, Lise, you've got a few more years, surely. Cheer up.'

'Non, j'en ai assez,' she says. 'Already. I've had enough.'

'Lise, don't cry.'

'Non, non, j'en ai assez.'

I also start to cry. No, life is too sad; it's quite impossible.

Sitting in front of the flamme bleue, arms round each other's waists, crying. No, life is too sad. ... My tears fall on her thick hair, which always smells so nice.

Enno, coming in with another bottle of Asti spumante, says: 'Oh, my God, this is gay,' and laughs loudly. Lise and I look at each other and start laughing too. Soon we are all rolling, helpless with laughter. It's too much, I can't any more, it's too much. ...

'Poor little Lise,' Enno says, 'she's a nice little girl, but too sentimental.'

Paulette is a very different matter. She is a gay, saucy wench, a great friend of Enno's. I admire and try to copy her and am jealous of her.

She reads us extracts from letters written to her by a lover in the provinces. ' "Tu es belle et tu sens bon." Well, what about it? And listen to this: "Your breasts fulfil the promise of your eyes." He's original, isn't he? And the two thousand francs I asked you for – where are they, vieux con? Never mind, he'll part before I've done with him. Wait a bit. Attends, mon salaud.'

One day they came back, Enno and Paulette, with a steak for me. They had had dinner out. I hadn't gone with them because I felt so sick, but that was over and I was hungry. Paulette cooked the steak over the flamme bleue and I ate it all up. 'Did you like it?' she said. 'Yes, I did.' 'You didn't notice anything about it?' 'I noticed it was a bit tough,' I said. 'Otherwise I liked it all right.' 'It was horse-steak,' she said. 'Oh, was it?' They were both watching me with narrowed eyes, expecting me to do the Anglaise stuff. But after I said: 'Oh, was it?' their mouths, that were wide open to laugh, went small again. After that I think Paulette knew I wasn't one of the comfortable ones, and never had been, and hadn't had such a grand time as all that. Afterwards she liked me better.

In the romantic tradition, Paulette. Long, yellow hair, soft, brown eyes, a bowl of violets in her room. When she looks at herself in the glass, naked, she's as proud as Lucifer. In the romantic tradition, and very generous. She brings me presents of silk stockings. She turns up with several pairs of socks for Enno. 'I've snaffled them,' she says. 'He won't know – he has too many.'

She tells us that one of her lovers, the Count of so-and-so, wants to marry her, but his family is shocked and horrified. 'Voilà,' says Paulette, 'je ne joue pas du piano, moi.' She is not bitter – she is regretful, fatalistic.

Besides, she has such bad luck – it's Fate. For instance, the other day the mother was actually persuaded to lunch with her. And what happened as they were walking out of the restaurant? Paulette's drawers fell off.

Do I believe this? Well, I believe that bit anyway, because exactly the same thing has happened to me.

Chuckling madly, on the bed in the hotel in the Rue Lamartine, and thinking of when that man said to me: 'Can you resist it?' 'Yes, I can,' I said, very coldly. I can resist it, just plain and Nordic like that, I certainly can.

'You must be mad,' he said, 'mad.' (Where is this happening? In Kensington.) The next thing he says is that he will see me to my bus. 'Stupid, stupid girl,' he says, doing up buttons, and he takes me to the bus stop. We are standing by a lamp-post, in dead silence, waiting for the bus, and what happens? My drawers fall off. I look down at them, step out of them neatly, pick them up, roll them into a little parcel and put them into my handbag. What else is there to do? He stares into vacancy, shocked beyond measure. The bus comes up. He lifts his hat with a flourish and walks away.

Next morning I realize that it is I who have lost ground. Decidedly. I feel awful about everything. I go to the nearest telephone and ring him up. 'Are you vexed with me about last night?' He answers: 'Yes, I am vexed, I am very vexed. ... I'll send you a box of Turkish Delight,' he says, and rings off.

Well, now, what is it, this Turkish Delight? Is it a comment, is it irony, is it compensation, is it apology, or what? I'll throw it out of the window, whatever it is.

•

Now snow is falling. There is the reflection of snow in the room. The light makes everything seem strange. The mound of my stomach is hidden under the bedclothes. So calm I feel, watching myself in the glass opposite. My hair hangs down on my shoulders. It is curly again and the corners of my mouth turn up. I like myself today. I am never sick now. I am very well and very happy. I never think of what it will be like to have this baby or, if I think, it's as if a door shuts in my head. Awful, terrible! And then a door shuts in your head.

I hardly ever think about money either, or that when it happens I may be alone. If the tea job comes off it won't do to risk losing it. So I may be in Paris alone.

But it's all arranged. As soon as it starts I am to get into a taxi and go off to the sage femme. My room is booked

– it's all arranged. It's nothing to make a fuss about, everybody says.

We are friendly with the patronne. She will keep an eye on me while Enno is away. I'll be all right.

The Russian for his lesson. I gave Enno a note putting him off – he must have forgotten to post it.

He looks surprised to find me in bed, the Russian – surprised, then cynical. Does he think it's all arranged, this being in bed? Does he think I want him to make love to me? But surely he can't think that. I believe he does, though.

The corners of his mouth go down when he says 'femme'. (Hatred or fear?) Les femmes – he doesn't trust them, they are capable of anything.

So calm I feel, amused as God, with the huge mound of my stomach safe under the bedclothes. ... It's no use arguing. As he's here, let's get on with it.

'I'm afraid this will have to be the last lesson,' I say.

The light makes everything seem strange. He kisses my hand, and I watch my hand as he kisses it – white, with red, varnished nails.

We are reading *Lady Windermere's Fan.*

'"The laughter, the horrible laughter of the world – a thing more tragic than all the tears the world has ever shed. ..." Will you stop me, please, if I mispronounce a word?'

The English conversation. ... He tells me about the Russian princess who was shut up in the prison of Peter and Paul to be eaten by rats, because she was a revolutionary. 'She screamed for ten days, and then there was silence. And then they let one day pass, and went into the cell. And there was nothing left of her but her hair. She had long and beautiful black hair.'

His conversation is nearly always about pain and torture.

He is going to join his family in London and then he is going up to Oxford. They have been very lucky. They have escaped with a good deal of money. The, this, that, these and those are all correct.

'Do you think English people will like me?'

'Yes, I'm certain they will.' (I've only got to look at you to know that they'll like you in England.)

'And my English?'

'But you speak English perfectly.'

He is pleased at this. He smirks. 'I try to keep in constant practice,' he says. He gives me the ten francs, kisses my hand again, bows from the waist and goes. Good-bye, dear sir, good-bye....

I put the ten francs under the pillow. I put the light out. While I can sleep, let me sleep. A boat rocking on a river, a smooth, green river. Outside, the secret streets. The man who sings, 'J'ai perdu la lumière....'

•

...The house in the Boulevard Magenta.

The sage femme has very white hands and clear, slanting eyes and when she looks at you the world stops rocking about. The clouds are clouds, trees are trees, people are people, and that's that. Don't mix them up again. No, I won't.

And there's always the tisane of orange-flower water.

But my heart, heavy as lead, heavy as a stone.

He has a ticket tied round his wrist because he died. Lying so cold and still with a ticket round his wrist because he died.

Not to think. Only to watch the branches of that tree and the pattern they make standing out against a cold sky. Above all, not to think....

When we got back to the hotel I felt very tired. I sat on the bed and looked down at the carpet. Except that I was tired I felt all right. But I kept thinking of the dress he had on – so pretty. It'll get all spoiled, I thought. Everything all spoiled.

'God is very cruel,' I said, 'very cruel. A devil, of

course. That accounts for everything – the only possible explanation.'

'I'm going out,' Enno said. 'I can't stay in here. I must go out.'

I stayed there, looking down at the dark red, dirty carpet and seeing a dark wall in the hot sun – the wall so hot it burned your hand when you touched it – and the red and yellow flowers and the time of day when every thing stands still.

*

Now the lights are red, dusky red, haggard red, cruel red. Strings plucked softly by a man with a long, thin nose and sharp, blue eyes.

Our luck has changed and the lights are red.

There we all are – Lise, Alfred, Jean. ... A fat man is shouting: 'La brune et la blonde, la brune et la blonde.' The cork of a champagne bottle pops. Why worry? Our luck has changed.

The fat man and I are in a corner by ourselves.

He says: 'Life is too awful. Do you know that story about the man who loved a woman who was married to somebody else, and she fell ill? And he didn't dare go and ask about her because the husband suspected her and hated him. So he just hung about the house and watched. And all the time he couldn't make up his mind whether he'd be a coward if he went and asked to see her or whether he'd be a coward if he didn't. And then one day he went and asked, and she was dead. Doesn't that make you laugh? She was dead, you see, and he had never sent one word. And he loved her and she was dying and he knew she was dying and he never sent one word. That's an old story, but doesn't it make you laugh? It might be true, that story, mightn't it?'

(Pourquoi êtes-vous, madame? Il ne faut pas être triste, madame. You mustn't be sad; you must laugh, you must dance. ...)

The fat man is still talking away.

'My partner has a very pretty wife and for some reason she was unhappy and so she went into the Bois de Boulogne and she walked a long way and got under a big tree. And there she put a revolver to her breast and pulled the trigger. Did she die? Of course not. Not a bit of it. If you really want to die you must put it into your mouth – up to the roof of your mouth. Well, she's still in the hospital. ... And just at first this made a great impression on my partner. He was in an awful state, thinking how unhappy she must have been to try to kill herself. But that was a week ago, and now he's just made up his mind that it's all a nuisance and that she made a fool of herself, and he's stopped being sorry for her. Isn't life droll?'

Well, there you are. It's not that these things happen or even that one survives them, but what makes life strange is that they are forgotten. Even the one moment that you thought was your eternity fades out and is forgotten and dies. This is what makes life so droll – the way you forget, and every day is a new day, and there's hope for everybody, hooray....

Now our luck has changed and the lights are red.

•

A room? A nice room? A beautiful room? A beautiful room with bath? Swing high, swing low, swing to and fro.... This happened and that happened....

And then the days came when I was alone.

•

'I'll write,' he said. 'I'll try to send you some money.'

But I knew it was finished. From the start I had known that one day this would happen – that we would say good-bye.

He leant out of the carriage window. I looked up at him and wondered if it were tears that made his eyes so bright. He wasn't one of those men who cry easily, Enno.

When the train had gone I had coffee in a bar near the Gare du Nord and looked through the window at the dark world and wide.

It's only for a time. We'll be together again when things go better. Knowing in myself that it was finished....

Did I love Enno at the end? Did he ever love me? I don't know. Only, it was after that that I began to go to pieces. Not all at once, of course. First this happened, and then that happened....

•

... I go to an hotel near the Place de la Madeleine. There are a lot of flies in this room. They torment me. I kill one. I didn't know flies have blood just like you or me. Well, there it lies, with its wings still and its legs turned up. You won't dance again....

I write to England, to try and borrow some money. They keep me waiting a long time for an answer and I start eating at a convent near by, where the nuns supply very cheap meals for destitute girls. She is kind, the old nun in charge, or she seems to me not unkind. The room where we eat looks on to a large stone courtyard. You can get a quarter of wine for a few sous.

But there's an English valet de chambre at the hotel who tells the patron that whatever I call myself now he had known me very well in London and that I had come to Paris with a great friend of his, a jockey, and that I had treated his friend very badly and that I was the dirtiest bitch he had ever struck, which was saying something. Useless to deny all this – quite useless. ... Was it hysteria, or a case of hate at first sight, or did he really mistake me for this other girl? I shall never know.

But he makes life hell for me, this valet de chambre.

At last the money comes from England. 'We can't go on doing this,' they say. 'You insisted on it against everybody's advice.' And so on. ... All right, I won't ask you again. A Spartan lot, they are.

I leave the hotel, I leave the quarter. For the last time I have washed my knife, fork and spoon and put them away in the locker. No more meals with the destitute girls.

But, after all, those were still the days when I went into a café to drink coffee, when I could feel gay on half a bottle of wine, when this happened and that happened.

But they never last, the golden days. And it can be sad, the sun in the afternoon, can't it? Yes, it can be sad, the afternoon sun, sad and frightening.

Now, money, for the night is coming. Money for my hair, money for my teeth, money for shoes that won't deform my feet (it's not so easy now to walk around in cheap shoes with very high heels), money for good clothes, money, money. The night is coming.

That's always when there isn't any. Just when you need it there's no money. *No money*. It gets you down.

Is it true that I am moche? God, no. I bet it was a woman said that. No, it wasn't. It was a man said it. Am I moche? No, no, you're young, you're beautiful.

Sometimes it's quite all right, sometimes it works. Often it works. And days. And nights....

Eat. Drink. Walk. March. Back to the hotel. To the Hotel of Arrival, the Hotel of Departure, the Hotel of the Future, the Hotel of Martinique and the Universe. ... Back to the hotel without a name in the street without a name. You press the button and the door opens. This is the Hotel Without-a-Name in the Street Without-a-Name, and the clients have no names, no faces. You go up the stairs. Always the same stairs, always the same room.

The room says: 'Quite like old times. Yes? ... No? ... Yes.'

*

After all this, what happened?

What happened was that, as soon as I had the slightest chance of a place to hide in, I crept into it and hid.

Well, sometimes it's a fine day, isn't it? Sometimes the skies are blue. Sometimes the air is light, easy to breathe. And there is always tomorrow. ...

Tomorrow I'll go to the Galeries Lafayette, choose a dress, go along to the Printemps, buy gloves, buy scent, buy lipstick, buy things costing fcs. 6.25 and fcs. 19.50, buy anything cheap. Just the sensation of spending, that's the point. I'll look at bracelets studded with artificial jewels, red, green and blue, necklaces of imitation pearls, cigarette-cases, jewelled tortoises. ... And when I have had a couple of drinks I shan't know whether it's yesterday, today or tomorrow.

Part Four

When I go into the bureau for my key the patronne tells me that an English monsieur has left a note for me. An English monsieur? ... Yes, that's what she understood – a monsieur from London.

Allo! Just dropped in to see you. Everything goes well with me. I have had enormous luck. I am leaving Paris tomorrow or the day after. So sorry I missed you.

RENÉ

As I get up to the fourth-floor landing the commis opens his door and puts his head out. 'Vache! Sale vache,' he says when he sees me. His head disappears and the door is slammed, but he goes on talking in a high, thin voice.

I take off my coat and hat and put away the scent and stockings I have just bought. All the time I am listening, straining my ears to hear what he is saying.

The voice stops. A loud knock. Now, this is too much, now I'm going to say a few things. If you think I'm afraid of you, you're mistaken. Wait a bit....

I march to the door and fling it open.

The gigolo is outside, looking excited and pleased with himself. He takes my hand in both of his.

'I came before. Did they tell you? ... But what's the matter? Why are you looking so frightened?'

'I'm not. I'm looking vexed.'

'Oh, no, you're looking frightened. Who are you frightened of? Me? But how flattering!'

'I thought it was the man next door. He's been shouting at me. He gets on my nerves.'

'He was rude to you? Voulez-vous que je lui casse la gueule?' he says.

'Certainly not. Not on any account.'

'I will if you wish. I can be useful in more ways than one.'

'Good God, no! Don't do anything of the sort.'

'Well, perhaps better not. I'd better not get into a row before I have my papers. But I shall have them. That's going to be all right tomorrow. ... I like this room,' he says. 'A nice room, a charming room. Nothing but beds. Can I sit down?'

'There are only two beds.'

'Ah, yes, so I see – only two. But somehow it gives the impression that it's full of beds. ... I waited up here for you nearly an hour this afternoon. I told your landlady I was a friend of yours from London. I spoke English to her. And she asked me if I'd like to wait in your room.'

I suppose this explains the 'Vache! Sale vache!'

'It's all very fine, but I asked you not to come up here and you said you wouldn't.'

'But why? The woman downstairs is so nice. ... I don't understand you. She doesn't mind in the least. You could have someone up here every hour and she wouldn't mind. It's a shame to waste this hotel, and this room. Very, very good to make love in, this room. Have you really been wasting it? I don't believe you have.' He laughs loudly. 'Those eyes, those deep shadows under your sad eyes – what about them?'

'Not what you think at all. I don't sleep well, and I take a lot of luminal to make me sleep.'

'Poor girl, poor girl,' he says, touching my eyes. 'And you won't let me even try to do anything about it?'

Now I am sick of being laughed at – sick, sick, sick of being laughed at. Allez-vous-en, salaud. I'm sick of being laughed at.

He feels that I am vexed. He says in a polite, formal voice: 'I came to ask you if you'd have an apéritif with me this evening. Please do. I shall be very disappointed if you can't.'

Very quick, very easy, that change of attitude, like a fish gliding with a flick of its tail, now here, now there.

'All right. I'll be at the Closerie des Lilas at half-past seven. I'm glad you've been lucky.'

'I've met an American,' he says mysteriously. 'Beautiful. And very, very rich. How do you say – bursting with it?'

'Lousy with it.'

'Yes, lousy with it.'

'Did you go to the Ritz bar?'

'No.'

'Don't tell me you met her at the Dôme?'

'Not the Dôme. That Danish place – you know. Well, we were talking and she said she wanted to go on somewhere else to dance. I said, quite frankly – Quite frank, you know. ...'

'I bet you were.'

'I said: "There's nothing I'd like better, nothing. But unfortunately at the moment I'm penniless – at least, almost penniless." After that it was all right. She's staying at the Meurice. It's been a great success.'

'Well, it's nice of you to come all the way over here to tell me about it.'

'That's just it. That's something you wouldn't understand. But when you're living like I do, you get very superstitious, and I think you bring me luck. Remember – that evening I met you. I was discouraged, very discouraged. You brought me luck.'

The luck-bringer. ... Well, I've never thought of myself in that way before.

He takes my hand in his and looks at my ring, his eyes narrowing.

'No good,' I say. 'Only worth about fifty francs – if that.'

'What, your hand?'

'You weren't looking at my hand, you were looking at my ring.'

'Oh, how suspicious she is, this woman! It's extraordinary.... But you will come this evening, won't you?'

'Yes, I'll be there. Where we talked the other night. I'll be there at half-past seven.'

He goes off, still looking triumphant.

I start walking up and down the room. I feel excited. I go to the glass, look at myself, stare at myself, make a grimace, look at my teeth. Damn this light – how can I see to make-up properly in this light?

Well, there I am, prancing about and smirking, and suddenly telling myself: 'No, I won't do a thing, not a thing. A little pride, a little dignity at the end, in the name of God. I won't even put on the stockings I bought this afternoon. I won't do a thing – not a thing. I will not grimace and posture before these people any longer.'

And, after all, the agitation is only on the surface. Underneath I'm indifferent. Underneath there is always stagnant water, calm, indifferent – the bitter peace that is very near to death, to hate....

I have sixteen hundred francs left. Enough to pay for the dress I chose today, enough to pay my hotel bill and the journey back to London. How much over? Say four hundred francs. I take two hundred and fifty. Two hundred francs for the meal, if there is a meal; fifty francs behind the mirror at the back of my handbag, for a taxi home in case we quarrel, in case he turns nasty. 'Hey, taxi' – and you're out of everything.

I time myself to be ten minutes late and arrive at the Closerie des Lilas at twenty minutes to eight. I look round the terrace. Nobody there. I won't go round the corner and look on the other side. He is sure to be indoors on such a cold night.

A very pretty girl is sitting on one of the stools at the bar, having a drink. No sign of the gigolo.

I order a Cinzano, feeling my pulse, as it were, all the

time. Am I disappointed, am I vexed? No, I am quite calm, also quite confident. He's somewhere around, I think.

I say to a waiter: 'Is there anybody on the terrace?'

'Oh, no, I don't think so. It's too cold tonight.'

'Would you go and have a look,' I say, quite calm, quite confident. 'And if there's anyone waiting, will you please tell him that I'm inside here.'

In a minute he comes back, followed by the gigolo.

'So here you are. I thought you'd stood me up.'

'I bet you thought the world had come to an end. I bet you couldn't believe it.'

'Well, no, I couldn't,' he says. 'But I was just beginning to believe it when the waiter came. I've been cursing you. You said where we talked the other night, and that's where I've been waiting. ... I'm cold. I've had two Pernods to keep me warm, but still I'm cold. Feel my hands. I'm going to have another Pernod.'

He looks a bit drunk, but drunk in the Latin way – very vivid, keyed-up.

The girl at the bar gets off her stool and walks out, passing slowly in front of us.

'Oh, what a beautiful girl! Look. Look at the way she walks – that movement of the hips. Oh, isn't she beautiful? What a lovely body that girl must have!'

'Wouldn't you like to go after her and find out?' I say. 'I rather think that was the idea.'

'No, no, it's you I want to talk to.'

'That's what I'm here for. Go ahead.'

'While we're having dinner,' he says. ... Pause of half a second for me to speak.

I ask him to have dinner with me.

'Thank you,' he says. 'To be frank, when I've paid for this lot of drinks I shan't have much money left.'

'What, haven't you got any money out of your American?'

'Oh no, not yet, not yet. When I ask her for something

it'll be something. But one mustn't do that too quickly, of course. She must be ready. ... She's nearly ready. I think perhaps tomorrow she'll be ready.'

He looks straight into my eyes all the time he is talking, with that air of someone defying you.

'Would you give me the money to pay for dinner now instead of in the restaurant?' he says, in the taxi. 'I'd prefer that.'

'Of course. I was going to.'

I give him the two hundred francs and the corners of his mouth go down.

'When you've settled up – dinner, drinks, taxis,' I say, 'there'll be about two francs left. I planned it out.'

'Oh, ce qu'elle est rosse, cette femme!'

I don't know what it is about this man that seems to me so natural, so gay – that makes me also feel natural and happy, just as if I were young – but really young. I've never been young. When I was young I was strained-up, anxious. I've never been really young. I've never played. ...

'I'm hungry,' he says. 'I'm so hungry that I can't think of anything but eating. To eat, to eat, and afterwards what's it matter?'

'This is another of my gay, chic places,' I say. 'You'll see, we'll have it all to ourselves.'

However, as it happens, there are several other people there, all eating seriously.

I want to see myself in a good light and I go upstairs to the lavabo, one of the attractions of the Pig and Lily. So clean and resplendent, so well lit, with plenty of looking-glasses and not a soul there to watch you. Am I looking all right? Not so bad. Surely, not so bad. ...

'At last,' he says when I come down. 'At last we are going to eat.'

I am not hungry. I expect he notices that the food isn't

at all good, in this damned boîte that isn't at all gay. However, he doesn't seem to notice. He eats a lot. He talks.

I don't believe in his American – he's probably invented her. And yet something must have happened to make him feel so pleased with himself and so sure of himself. Also he seems certain that he will be in London in a few days.

He tries to get useful information from me. Night clubs, for instance, restaurants. Which are the ones to go to? Everything is clubs in London, isn't it? Clubs, clubs. ... Yes, everything is clubs, clubs, clubs, clubs, clubs in London. ... How can he find a really chic tailor? Do the good ones advertise?

'I don't know. I'm the wrong person to ask all this.'

'Couldn't you give a party and introduce me to your friends?' Half-mocking, half-wheedling.

'I haven't any friends.'

'Ah, too bad, too bad.'

He has never been to London, it seems, but he knows all about it. He has been told this and he has been told that.

By the time we have started on the second bottle of wine I have heard all about the gold-mine just across the Channel.

A curious situation – according to his friends. At least fifty per cent of the men homosexual and most of the others not liking it so much as all that. And the poor Englishwomen just gasping for it, oh, boy! And aren't they prepared to pay, if you go about it the right way, oh, boy! A curious situation.

The untapped gold-mine just across the Channel. ...

I am eating very little, so the wine has an effect, and I begin to argue with this optimistic idiot.

But at the end of my arguments he says calmly: 'You talk like that because you're a woman, and everybody knows England isn't a woman's country. You know the proverb – "Unhappy as a dog in Turkey or a woman in England"? But for me it will be different.'

That's his idea. But he'll find out that he will be up against racial, not sexual, characteristics. Love is a stern virtue in England. (Usually a matter of hygiene, my dear. The indecent necessity – and who would spend money or thought or time on the indecent necessity? ... We have our ration of rose-leaves, but only because rose-leaves are a gentle laxative.)

'You take care. You'll probably get a cigarette case en toc with your initials on it after a lot of hard work.'

He's so sure that everything is going to be all right, you have to be sorry for him. And he's so good-looking, this poor devil, so alive, gay, healthy, so as if he didn't drink much, so as if. ... Talking away about the technique of the métier – it sounds quite meaningless. It probably is meaningless. He's just trying to shock me or excite me or something. ...

It's half-past nine. There we still sit, jabbering.

'Is it true that Englishmen make love with all their clothes on, because they think it's more respectable that way?'

'Yes, certainly. Fully dressed. They add, of course, a macintosh.'

After this we are properly off.

'Now I'll show you something really funny,' he says. 'Look at this in the spoon. ...'

'Yes. It is rather funny, isn't it?'

'I can do better than that,' he says.

I watch very carefully. If I learn this trick, it ought to raise my amusement-value.

Do you like this? Do you like that? What do you really like worse than anything else? I'll tell you something very curious I heard of the other day. Etcetera, etcetera. ...

He is very good at this – calm, indifferent, without a

glint in his eye. But his voice gets louder. Happily there is only one lot of people left in the room, and I don't think they understand English.

But the proprietor certainly understands. When he comes up with the coffee he looks at me in a half-pitying, half-severe way, as if to say: 'Really, really, really. ... I should have thought you'd have more sense than this. Really, really. ...' He certainly does understand English.

I stare back at him. Well, and what about it, you damned old goop? Are you as blameless as all that? Are you? I shouldn't think so. I don't criticize you, so don't you criticize me. See?

He walks away in a dignified manner. 'Tous piqués,' he is thinking, 'tous dingo, tous, tous, tous. ...'

All the same, this conversation is becoming a bit of a strain. What is it leading up to? ... Ah! here it comes.

'I've arranged everything. While I was waiting for you on the terrace I asked the waiter to tell me a place I could take you to as you said you didn't want to go back to your hotel with me. He told me of a very good place in the Boulevard Raspail.'

'My God!' I say. 'You asked the waiter?'

'Yes, of course. Waiters always know about that sort of thing.'

'Well, that's somewhere else I'll never be able to show my face in again.'

'And then you say you're not a bourgeoise!'

'I didn't say that. You said it.'

All the same, he's quite right. Tomorrow I must walk into that café and go to that same table on the terrace and have a drink. But when I think 'tomorrow' there is a gap in my head, a blank – as if I were falling through emptiness. Tomorrow never comes.

I say: 'Tomorrow never comes.'

'I don't understand.'

'Listen. I've told you this from the start – nothing doing. Why do you go on about it? It's stupid.'

'A pity,' he says, indifferently, 'a pity. It would have been so nice. You wouldn't have been disappointed in me.'

(But supposing you were disappointed in me.)

He's clever, this man, he feels what I am thinking. He says: 'You know, you needn't be afraid of me. I'd never say cruel things to you, nor about you either. I'm not cruel to women – not in that way. You see, I like them. I don't like boys; I tried in Morocco, but it was no use. I like women.'

'Then you ought to be worth your weight in gold. I only hope you get it.'

'Do you like girls?' he says, looking inquisitive.

'No, I don't.'

'What, have you never in your life seen a girl you could have loved?'

'No, never. ... Yes, once I did. I saw a girl in a bordel I could have loved.'

'Oh, how convenient!'

He laughs. The proprietor starts, looks towards us, shrugs his shoulders and turns his back.

'Why did you love her?'

'Well,' I say, 'what a question, anyway!'

How on earth can you say why you love people? You might as well say you know where the lightning is going to strike. At least, that's how it has always seemed to me.

'Tell me about this girl.'

'There isn't anything to tell, except that I liked her. She looked awfully sad and very gentle. That doesn't happen often.'

He seems much amused.

'Did she make love to you?'

'No, of course not,' I say. 'Certainly not.'

'What happened? Do tell me.'

'Well, while I was thinking these sentimental thoughts a fresh client came in and she rushed off to join the crowd that was twittering round him. You know how they do. ... I loathe bordels, anyway.'

(Now, why has this girl suddenly come up out of the past? She wasn't beautiful, not a star at all. I expect she didn't have a very good time. But I wanted to put my arms round her, kiss her eyes and comfort her – and if that's not love, what is?)

'Oh, all women hate bordels,' he says.

'Oh yeah? Well, you wouldn't think so to hear some of them talk. Besides, don't tell me that I'm like other women – I'm not.'

'Yes, but all women say that too,' he says.

Now it seems to me that there is antagonism in the air. It would be a pity if we ended with a quarrel.

'I'm no use to anybody,' I say. 'I'm a cérébrale, can't you see that?'

Thinking how funny a book would be, called 'Just a Cérébrale or You Can't Stop Me From Dreaming'. Only, of course, to be accepted as authentic, to carry any conviction, it would have to be written by a man. What a pity, what a pity!

'Is that your idea of yourself?' he says.

'It is, certainly.'

'It's not mine at all. I should have thought you were rather stupid.'

This pulls me up short. If he thinks me stupid now I wonder what he would say to my usual conversation, which goes like this: 'I believe it's going to be fine today – yes, I hope it is – yes – yes – yes –'

'You think me stupid?' I say.

'No, no. Don't be vexed. I don't mean stupid. I mean that you feel better than you think.'

Do I? I wonder. ... Oh well, stupid. ... An extremely funny monologue is going on in my head – or it seems to me extremely funny. I want to stop myself from laughing out loud, so I say: 'We're getting very high-toned. What is a cérébrale, anyway! I don't know. Do you?'

'A cérébrale,' he says, seriously, 'is a woman who doesn't like men or need them.'

'Oh, is that it? I've often wondered. Well, there are quite a lot of those, and the ranks are daily increasing.'

'Ah, but a cérébrale doesn't like women either. Oh, no. The true cérébrale is a woman who likes nothing and nobody except herself and her own damned brain or what she thinks is her brain.'

So pleased with herself, like a little black boy in a top-hat....

'In fact, a monster.'

'Yes, a monster.'

'Well, after all that it's very comforting to know that you think I'm stupid.... Let's ask for the bill, shall we? Let's go.'

'I rang you up the other morning,' he says.

'Yes, I know. I was asleep. I got down to the telephone too late.'

'You knew who it was?'

'Oh, I thought it might be you. I wasn't sure.'

'You have friends in Paris, then?'

'I don't know a soul here, except two Russians I met the other day. I like them very much.'

'Russians,' he says in a spiteful voice, 'Russians in Paris! Everybody knows what they are – Jews and poor whites. The most boring people in the world. Terrible people.'

For some reason I am very vexed at this. I start wondering why I am there at all, what I am doing in this box of a restaurant, swapping dirty stories with a damned gigolo. I want to get away. I want to be out of the place.

'I'm going to the Exhibition,' I say. 'I want to see it again at night before I go.'

'The Exhibition?'

'Haven't you been to it?'

'No, I haven't. What should I do at the Exhibition?'

'Well, I'm going. You needn't come if you don't want to. I'll go by myself.'

I want to go by myself, to get into a taxi and drive along the streets, to stand by myself and look down at the fountains in the cold light.

'But of course,' he says. 'If you want to go to the Exhibition, we'll go. Naturally.'

*

We go in by the Trocadéro entrance. There aren't many people about. Cold, empty, beautiful – this is what I imagined, this is what I wanted.

'What's that light up there?' he says.

'That's the Star of Peace. Don't you recognize it?'

He stares back at it.

'How mesquin! It's vulgar, that Star of Peace.'

'The building is very fine,' I say, in a schoolmistress's voice.

We stand on the promenade above the fountains, looking down on them. This is what I wanted – the cold fountains, the cold, rainbow lights on the water....

He says again: 'It's mesquin, your Star of Peace.'

We stand for some time, leaning over the balustrade. He puts his arm through mine. I can feel him shivering. When I tell him so he answers: 'Well, it's cold here after Morocco.'

'Oh yes, of course. Morocco.'

'You don't believe I've come from Morocco, do you?'

Whatever else is a lie about him, it's certainly true that he isn't dressed for this weather.

The lights shimmering on the water, the leaping fountains, cold and beautiful....

'Why don't you borrow some money from your American and buy yourself an overcoat?'

'No, I'm going to wait. I want to get my clothes in London.'

For God's sake – he's going to start up again about the addresses of London tailors....

'Let's go and have a drink somewhere. That'll make us warm.'

'A drink?' he says. 'Oh yes, of course. But supposing I don't want to walk a long way in the cold just to get a cheap drink.'

He begins to whistle, like a little boy whistles when he is trying to keep his courage up – loud, clear and pure.

'What's that tune? I like it.'

'That's the march of the Legion,' he says, 'the real one. Or that's what I think it is. But how should I know.'

'Tell me about Morocco.'

'No, I don't want to talk about it. ... I don't want to think about it,' he says loudly. 'Come on, let's go and have our drink.'

'The good-bye one,' I say.

'All right – the good-bye one. But not in here. Let's get out of here....'

We sit side by side in the taxi, not touching each other. He is whistling softly all the time. I watch the streets through the window. Well, there you are, Paris, and this is the good-bye drink....

'Where are we going?' he says.

We are passing the Deux Magots.

'This is all right. Let's go in here.'

The café is not very full. I choose a table as far away from everyone else as possible. We order two brandies.

He has told me that he is twenty-six, but I think he is older than that – he's about thirty. And he doesn't look like a gigolo, not at all like a gigolo.

Suddenly I feel shy and self-conscious. (How ridiculous! Don't let him see it, for God's sake.) I drink half my brandy-and-soda and start talking about the last time I was in the Deux Magots and how I had been staying at

Antibes and how I came back very brown and on top of the world and with some money too, and all the rest.

'Money I had earned. Sans blague. It was too funny. I wrote up fairy stories for a very rich woman. She came to Montparnasse looking for somebody and of course there was a rush. She chose me because I was the cheapest. The night I got back to Montparnasse – very rich – we celebrated. We started up in this café because I was staying at a hotel near here.'

What with the brandy-and-soda and going back to the Deux Magots, the whole thing is whirling nicely round in my head. She would come into my room very early in the morning in her dressing-gown, her hair hanging down in two plaits, looking rather sweet, I must say. 'Are you awake, Mrs Jansen? I've just thought of a story. You can take it down in shorthand, can't you?' 'No, I'm afraid I can't.' (Cheated! For what I'm paying she ought to know shorthand.) 'But if you'll tell me what you want to say I think I can get it down.' Off she'd go. 'Once upon a time there was a cactus –' Or a white rose or a yellow rose or a red rose, as the case might be. All this, mind you, at six-thirty in the morning. ... 'This story,' she would say, looking anxious, 'is an allegory. You understand that, don't you?' 'Yes, I understand.' But she was never very explicit about the allegory. 'Could you make it a Persian garden?' 'I don't see why not.' 'Oh, and there's something I want to speak to you about, Mrs Jansen. I'm afraid Samuel didn't like the last story you wrote.' Oh God, this awful sinking of the heart – like going down in a lift. I knew this job was too good to be true. 'Didn't he? I'm sorry. What didn't he like about it?' 'Well, I'm afraid he doesn't like the way you write. What he actually said was that, considering the cost of these stories, he thinks it strange that you should write them in words of one syllable. He says it gets monotonous, and don't you know any long words, and if you do, would you please use them? ... Madame Holmberg is most anxious to collaborate with me. And she's a real writer – she's just finished the third volume of her Life of Napoleon.' After this delicate hint she adds: 'Samuel wished to speak to you himself, but I told him that I preferred to do it, because I didn't want to hurt your feelings. I said I was sure, if I told you his opinion, you'd try to do better. I should hate to hurt your feelings because in a strange way I feel that we are very much alike. Don't you think so?' (No, I certainly don't think so, you pampered chow.) 'I'm awfully sorry you didn't like the story,' I say.

Sitting at a large desk, a white sheet of paper in front of me and outside the sun and the blue Mediterranean. Monte Carlo, Monte Carlo, by the Med-it-er-rany-an sea-ee, Monte Carlo, Monte Carlo, where the boy of my heart waits for me-ee. ... Persian garden. Long words. Chiaroscuro? Translucent? ... I bet he'd like cataclysmal action and centrifugal flux, but the point is how can I get them into a Persian garden? ... Well, I might. Stranger things have happened. ... A blank sheet of paper. ... Once upon a time, once upon a time there lived a lass who tended swine. ... Persian gardens. Satraps – surely they were called satraps. ... It's so lovely outside, and music has started up somewhere. ... Grinding it out, oh God, with all the long words possible. And the music outside playing *Valencia*. ... 'Are you still there, Mrs Jansen? You haven't gone out? I've just thought of a new story. Once upon a time there lived....'

Shrewd as they're born, this woman, hard as a nail, and with what a sense of property! She'd raise hell if a spot of wine fell on one of her Louis Quinze chairs. Authentic Louis Quinze, of course they were.

They explain people like that by saying that their minds are in water-tight compartments, but it never seemed so to me. It's all washing about, like the bilge in the hold of a ship, all washing around in the same hold – no water-tight compartments. ... Fairies, red roses, the sense of property – Of course they don't feel things like we do – Lilies in the moonlight – I believe in survival after death. I've had personal proof of it. And we'll find our dear, familiar bodies on the other side – Samuel has forgotten to buy his suppositoires – Pity would be out of place in this instance – I never take people like that to expensive restaurants. Quite unnecessary and puts ideas into their heads. It's not *kind*, really – Nevertheless, all the little birdies sing – Psycho-analysis might help. Adler is more wholesome than Freud, don't you think? – English judges never make a mistake – The piano is quite Egyptian in feeling....

All washing around in the same hold. No water-tight compartments....

Well, I am trying to tell René about all this and giggling a good deal, when he stops me.

'But I know that woman. I know her very well. ... Again you don't believe me. This time you shall believe me. Listen, she was like this –' He describes her exactly. 'And the house was like this –' He draws a little plan on the back of an envelope. 'Here are the palm trees. Here are the entrance steps. That terrible English butler they had – do you remember? The two cabinets here with jade, the other two cabinets with a collection of china. The double circular staircase – do you remember how they used to come down it at night?'

'Yes,' I say. '"I know how to walk down a staircase, me."'

'Which bedroom did you have? Did you have the one on the second floor with the green satin divan in the antechamber to the bathroom?'

'No. I had a quite ordinary one on the third floor. But what an array of scent-bottles! I dream of them sometimes.'

'It was a ridiculous house, wasn't it?'

'I was very much impressed,' I say. 'It's the only millionaire's house I've ever stayed in in my life.'

'I've stayed in much richer ones than that. I've stayed

in one so rich that when you pulled the lavatory-plug it played a tune. ... Rich people – you have to be sorry for them. They haven't the slightest idea how to spend their money; they haven't the slightest idea how to enjoy themselves. Either they have no taste at all, or, if they have any taste, it's like a mausoleum and they're shut up in it.'

'Well you're going to alter all that, aren't you?'

Of course, there's no doubt that this man has stayed in this house and does know these people. One would think that that would give us more confidence in each other. Not at all, it makes us suspicious. There's no doubt that a strict anonymity is a help on these occasions.

When did all this happen, and what is his story? Did he stay in France for a time, get into trouble over here and then join the Legion? Is that the story? Well, anyway, what's it matter to me what his story is? I expect he has a different one every day.

I say: 'Excuse me a minute,' primly, and go down to the lavatory.

This is another lavatory that I know very well, another of the well-known mirrors.

'Well, well,' it says, 'last time you looked in here you were a bit different, weren't you? Would you believe me that, of all the faces I see, I remember each one, that I keep a ghost to throw back at each one – lightly, like an echo – when it looks into me again?' All glasses in all lavabos do this.

But it's not as bad as it might be. This is just the interval when drink makes you look nice, before it makes you look awful.

He says: 'You're always disappearing into the lavabo, you. C'est agaçant.'

'What do you expect?' I say, staring at him. 'I'm getting old.'

He frowns. 'No, don't say that. Don't talk like that. You're not old. But you've got to where you're afraid to be young. I know. They've frightened you, haven't they? Why do you let them frighten you? They always try to do that, if it isn't in one way it's in another.'

'Thanks for the good advice. I'll try to remember it. Now I'm all ready for another *fine*.'

'But you said that if you drink too much you cry. And I have a horror of people who cry when they're drunk.'

'I don't feel a bit like that. Never happier in my life.'

He looks at me and says: 'No, I don't think you are going to cry. All right.'

And here's another brandy. I squirt the soda in and watch the bubbles rising up from the bottom of the glass. I'll drink it slowly, this one.

'Well, don't be too long. Finish that, and then we'll go.'

'Where to?'

'Well, to your hotel or to the Boulevard Raspail. Just as you like. ... You're such a stupid woman,' he says, 'such a stupid woman. Why do you go on pretending? Now, look me straight in the eyes and say you don't want to.'

'Of course I do.'

'Then why won't you? At least tell me why you won't. Something that you would like and that I would like –'

'Something so unimportant.'

'Oh, important!' he says. 'But it would be nice. At least tell me why you won't, or is that too much to ask?'

'Oh no, it's not too much to ask. I'll tell you. It's because I'm afraid.'

'Afraid,' he says, 'afraid! But what are you afraid of? ... You think I'll strangle you, or cut your throat for the sake of that beautiful ring of yours. Is that it?'

'No, I'm sure you wouldn't kill me to get my ring.'

'Then perhaps you are afraid I'll kill you, not because I want money, but because I like to do bad things. But that's where you're so stupid. With you, I don't want to do bad things.'

'There's always the one that you don't want to do bad things with, isn't there?'

'Yes, there's always the one,' he says. 'I want to lie close to you and feel your arms round me.'

– And tell me everything, everything. ... He has said that bit before.

'Oh, stop talking about it.'

'Of course,' he says. 'But first, just as a matter of curiosity, I'd like to know what you are so afraid of. Finish your drink and tell me. Just as a matter of curiosity.'

I drink. Something in his voice has hurt me. I can't say anything. My throat hurts and I can't say anything.

'You are afraid of me. You think I'm méchant. You do think I might kill you.'

If I thought you'd kill me, I'd come away with you right now and no questions asked. And what's more, you could have any money I've got with my blessing. ...

'I don't think you're any more méchant than anybody else. Less, probably.'

'Then what are you afraid of? Tell me. I'm interested. Of men, of love? ... What, still? ... Impossible.'

You are walking along a road peacefully. You trip. You fall into blackness. That's the past – or perhaps the future. And you know that there is no past, no future, there is only this blackness, changing faintly, slowly, but always the same.

'You want to know what I'm afraid of? All right, I'll tell you. ... I'm afraid of men – yes, I'm very much afraid of men. And I'm even more afraid of women. And I'm very much afraid of the whole bloody human race. ... Afraid of them?' I say. 'Of course I'm afraid of them. Who wouldn't be afraid of a pack of damned hyenas?'

Thinking: 'Oh, shut up. Stop it. What's the use?' But I can't stop. I go on raving.

'And when I say afraid – that's just a word I use. What I really mean is that I hate them. I hate their voices, I hate their eyes, I hate the way they laugh. ... I hate the whole bloody business. It's cruel, it's idiotic, it's unspeakably horrible. I never had the guts to kill myself or I'd have got out of it long ago. So much the worse for me. Let's leave it at that.'

... I know all about myself now, I know. You've told me so often. You haven't left me one rag of illusion to clothe myself in. But by God, I know what you are too, and I wouldn't change places....

Everything spoiled, all spoiled. Well, don't cry about it. No, I won't cry about it. ... But may you tear each other to bits, you damned hyenas, and the quicker the better. ... Let it be destroyed. Let it happen. Let it end, this cold insanity. Let it happen.

Only five minutes ago I was in the Deux Magots, dressed in that damned cheap black dress of mine, giggling and talking about Antibes, and now I am lying in a misery of utter darkness. Quite alone. No voice, no touch, no hand. ... How long must I lie here? For ever? No, only for a couple of hundred years this time, miss....

I heave myself out of the darkness slowly, painfully. And there I am, and there he is, the poor gigolo.

He looks sad. He says, speaking in a low voice and for the first time with a very strong accent: 'I have wounds,' pronouncing 'wounds' so oddly that I don't understand what he means.

'You have what?'

I look round. Have I screamed, shouted, cursed, cried, made a scene? Is anyone looking at us, is anyone noticing us? No, nobody. ... The woman at the desk is sitting with her eyes cast down. I notice the exact shade of the blue eye-shadow on her lids. They must see the start of some funny things, these women perched up in cafés, perched up like idols. Especially the ones at the Dôme.

'You have what?'

'Look,' he says, still speaking in a whisper. He throws his head up. There is a long scar, going across his throat.

Now I understand what it means – from ear to ear. A long, thick, white scar. It's strange that I haven't noticed it before.

He says: 'That is one. There are other ones. I have been wounded.'

It isn't boastful, the way he says this, nor complaining. It's puzzled, puzzled in an impersonal way, as if he is asking me – me, of all people – why, why, why?

Pity you? Why should I pity you? Nobody has ever pitied me. They are without mercy.

'I have too,' I say in a surly voice. 'Moi aussi.'

'I know. I can see that. I believe you.'

'Well,' I say, 'if we're going to start believing each other, it's getting serious, isn't it?'

I want to get out of this dream.

'But why shouldn't we believe each other? Why shouldn't we believe each other just for tonight? Will you believe something I'm going to say to you now? I want absolutely to make love to you.'

'I told you from the start you were wasting your time.'

'What happened to you, what happened?' he says. 'Something bad must have happened to make you like this.'

'One thing? It wasn't one thing. It took years. It was a slow process.'

He says: 'It doesn't matter. What I know is that I could do this with you' – he makes a movement with his hands like a baker kneading a loaf of bread – 'and afterwards you'd be different. I know. Believe me.'

I watch the little grimacing devil in my head. He wears a top-hat and a cache-sexe and he sings a sentimental song – 'The roses all are faded and the lilies in the dust.'

I say: 'Now who's trying to make an unimportant thing sound important?'

'Oh, important, unimportant – that's just words. If we can be happy for a little, forget everything for a little, isn't that important enough? ... Now we'll go. We'll go back to your hotel.'

'No.'

Leave me alone. I'm tired....

'Still rien à faire?' He starts to laugh.

'Still rien à faire. Absolutely rien à faire.'

But everything is so changed, I can't look at him.

'I must go. Please. I'm so tired.'

In the taxi I say: 'Whistle that tune, will you? The one you said is the march of the Legion.'

He whistles it very softly. And I watch the streets through the window. À l'Hôtel de l'Espérance....

*

I am in a little whitewashed room. The sun is hot outside. A man is standing with his back to me, whistling that tune and cleaning his shoes. I am wearing a black dress, very short, and heel-less slippers. My legs are bare. I am watching for the expression on the man's face when he turns round. Now he ill-treats me, now he betrays me. He often brings home other women and I have to wait on them, and I don't like that. But as long as he is alive and near me I am not unhappy. If he were to die I should kill myself.

My film-mind. ... ('For God's sake watch out for your film-mind. ...')

'What are you laughing at now?' he says.

'Nothing, nothing. ... I do like that tune. Do you think I could get a gramophone record of it?'

'I don't know.'

We are at the door of the hotel.

'Good night,' he says. 'Sleep well. Take a big dose of luminal.'

'I will. And the same to you.'

I am not sad as I go upstairs, not sad, not happy, not

regretful, not thinking of anything much. Except that I see very clearly in my head the tube of luminal and the bottle of whisky. In case....

Just as I have got to my door there is a click and everything is in darkness. Impossible to get the key in. I must cross the pitch-black landing to the head of the stairs and put the time-switch on again.

I am feeling for the knob when I see the light of a cigarette a yard or two from my face. I stand for what seems a long while watching it. Then I call out: 'Who is it? Who's there? Qui est là?'

But before he answers I know. I take a step forward and put my arms round him.

I have my arms round him and I begin to laugh, because I am so happy. I stand there hugging him, so terribly happy. Now everything is in my arms on this dark landing – love, youth, spring, happiness, everything I thought I had lost. I was a fool, wasn't I? to think all that was finished for me. How could it be finished?

I put up my hand and touch his hair. I've wanted to do that ever since I first saw him.

'Did I frighten you at first?'

He has put the light on. He looks pleased, but surprised.

'No, no,' I say. 'Yes, a bit.... No.'

But I whisper and look round fearfully. What do I expect to see? There is nobody on the landing – nothing. Nothing but the commis' shoes by his door, the toes carefully pointed outwards as usual.

He takes the key from my hand, opens the door and shuts it after us. We kiss each other fervently, but already something has gone wrong. I am uneasy, half of myself somewhere else. Did anybody hear me, was anybody listening just now?

'It's dark in here.... Just a minute, I'll fix it.'

The switch in my room works either the light near the bed or the one over the curtained wash-basin – it depends on how far the knob is pushed. But it is always going wrong and doing one thing when you expect it to do another. I fumble with it for some time before I can get the lamp near the bed going.

Now the room springs out at me, laughing, triumphant. The big bed, the little bed, the table with the tube of luminal, the glass and the bottle of Evian, the two books, the clock ticking on the ledge, the menu – 'T'as compris? Si, j'ai compris. ...' Four walls, a roof and a bed. *Les Hommes en Cage*.... Exactly.

Here we are. Nothing to stop us. Four walls, a roof, a bed, a bidet, a spotlight that goes on first over the bidet and then over the bed – nothing to stop us. Anything you like; anything you like. ... No past to make us sentimental, no future to embarrass us. ... A difficult moment when you are out of practice – a moment that makes you go cold, cold and wary.

'Would you like some whisky?' I say. 'I've got some.'

(That's original. I bet nobody's ever thought of that way of bridging the gap before.)

I take my coat and hat off, get the bottle of whisky. I rinse the tooth-glass out, mix myself a drink and mix one for him in the Evian glass, which is clean. I do all this as slowly as possible. Time, time, give me time – wait a minute, wait a minute, not yet....

We sit on the small bed. He takes one sip of whisky and puts the glass away.

'Isn't it right? Don't you like it?'

'Yes, it's all right. I don't want to drink.'

'Mine tastes awful. It tastes of mouthwash.'

'Then why do you drink it? Don't drink it.'

All the same, I go on sipping away. Small sips. Not yet, not yet. ... Wait a minute. ... You won't be unkind, will you? For God's sake, say something kind to me. ... But his eyes are ironical as he watches me. I don't think he is going to say anything kind. On the contrary. But that's natural. I've got to expect that. Technique.

I say: 'It's funny how some men try to get you to swill as much as you can hold, and others try to stop you. Automatically. Some profound instinct seems to get going. Something racial – yes, I'm sure it's racial.'

He says: 'Just now on the landing – you knew it was me?'

'Yes, of course.'

'But how could you have known before I said anything?'

'I did know,' I say obstinately.

'Then you knew that I was coming up after you. You expected me to?'

'Oh no, I didn't. I didn't a bit.'

He laughs and puts his hand on my knee under my dress. I hate that. It reminds me of – Never mind. ...

'You love playing a comedy, don't you?'

'How do you mean – a comedy?'

I shouldn't have taken whisky on top of brandy. It's making me feel quarrelsome. Sparks of anger, or resentment, shooting all over me. ... A comedy, what comedy? A comedy, my God!

The damned room grinning at me. The clock ticking. Qu'est-ce qu'elle fout ici, la vieille?

'I'm going to have another whisky.'

'No, don't drink any more.'

Oh, go to hell. ... I push his hand away and get up.

'Tell me something. You think that I meant you all the time to come up here, and that everything else I said this evening was what you call a comedy?'

'I knew you really wanted me to come up – yes. That was easy to see,' he says.

I could kill him for the way he said that, and for the way he is looking at me. ... Easy, easy, free and easy. Easy to fool, easy to torture, easy to laugh at. But not again. Oh no, not again. ... You've been unkind too soon. Bad technique.

'Hooray,' I say, 'here's to you. It was sweet of you to

come up and I was very pleased to see you. Now you've got to go.'

'Of course I'm not going. Why are you like this? Don't be like this.'

'No, it's no use. I'd rather you went.'

'Well, I'm not going,' he says. 'I want to see this comedy. You'll have to call for someone to put me out.... Au secours, au secours,' he shouts in a high falsetto voice. 'Like that.... If you want to make yourself ridiculous.'

'I've been so ridiculous all my life that a little bit more or a little bit less hardly matters now.'

'Call out, then. Go on. Or why don't you rap on the wall and ask your friend next door to help you?'

As soon as he says this I am very quiet. If there is one thing on earth I want to avoid, it is a scene in this hotel.

'I don't want to have a row here,' I say. 'Only you've got to go.'

'Why?'

'Well, because I tell you to go. And you'll go.'

'Just like that?'

'Yes, just like that.'

'But what do you think I am – a little dog? You think you can first kiss me and then say to me "Get out"? You haven't looked well at me.... I don't like it,' he says, 'that voice that gives orders.'

Well, I haven't always liked it, either – the voice that gives orders.

'Very well, I ask you to go.'

'Oh, you annoy me,' he says. 'You annoy me, you annoy me.'

And there we are – struggling on the small bed. My idea is not so much to struggle as to make it a silent struggle. Nobody must hear us. At the end, he is lying on me, holding down my two spread arms. I can't move. My dress is torn open at the neck. But I have my knees firmly clamped together. This is a game – a game played in the snow for a worthless prize....

He is breathing quickly and I can feel his heart beating. I am quite calm. 'This is really a bit comic,' I keep thinking. Also I think: 'He looks méchant, he could be méchant, this man.'

I shut my eyes because I want to stay calm, I want to be able to keep thinking: 'This is really damned comic.'

'We're on the wrong bed,' I say. 'And with all our clothes on, too. Just like English people.'

'Oh, we have a lot of time. We have all night. We have till tomorrow.'

A long time till tomorrow. A hundred years, perhaps, till tomorrow....

'There's a very good truc,' he says, 'for women like you, who pretend and lie and play an idiotic comedy all the time.'

He tells me about it.

'Very good, very good. Where did you learn that? In Morocco?'

'Oh no,' he says, 'in Morocco it's much easier. You get four comrades to help you, and then it's very easy. They each take their turn. It's nice like that.' He laughs loudly.

'For goodness' sake,' I say – 'you can describe your charming methods without shouting at the top of your voice, surely.'

'You think you're very strong, don't you?' he says.

'Yes, I'm very strong.'

I'm strong as the dead, my dear, and that's how strong I am.

'If you're so strong, why do you keep your eyes shut?'

Because dead people must have their eyes shut.

I lie very still, I don't move. Not open my eyes....

'Je te ferai mal,' he says. 'It's your fault.'

When I open my eyes I feel the tears trickling down from the outside corners.

'That's better, that's better. Now say "I tell you to go, and you'll go".'

I can't speak.

'That's better, that's better.'

I feel his hard knee between my knees. My mouth hurts, my breasts hurt, because it hurts, when you have been dead, to come alive....

'Now everything's going to be all right,' he says.

'T'as compris?' he says.

Of course, the ritual answer is 'Si, j'ai compris....'

I lie there, thinking 'Yes, I understand'. Thinking 'For the last time'. Thinking nothing. Listening to a high, clear, cold voice. My voice.

'Of course I understand. Naturally I understand. I should be an awful fool if I didn't. If you look in the right-hand pocket of the dressing-case over on that table you'll find the money you want.'

He lets go of my wrists. I feel him go very still.

'It isn't locked. Take the thousand-franc note. But for God's sake leave me the others, or I'll be in an awful jam.'

But how heavy he is, how much heavier than one would have thought....

'You mustn't think,' I say, 'that I'm vexed about anything, because I'm not. Everybody's got their living to earn, haven't they? I'm just trying to save you a lot of trouble.'

Don't listen, that's not me speaking. Don't listen. Nothing to do with me – I swear it....

'And I thought you were awfully sweet to me,' I say. 'I loved all the various stories you told me about yourself. Especially that one about your wounds and your scars – that amused me very much.'

I put my arm up over my face, because I have a feeling that he is going to hit me.

'I'm just trying to save you a whole lot of trouble,' I say, 'a whole lot of waste of time. You can have the money right away, so it would be a waste of time, wouldn't it?'

His weight is not on me any longer. He is standing up. He has moved so quickly that I haven't had time to put my arms round him, or to say 'Stay', to say 'Don't do this, don't leave me like this, don't.'

'Yes, you're right,' he says. 'It would be a waste of time.'

'You and your wounds – don't you see how funny you are? You did make me laugh. Other people's wounds – how funny they are! I shall laugh every time I think about you....'

I keep my arm over my eyes. He is walking over to the glass, looking at himself, putting his tie straight. Now he is opening the dressing-case. I keep my arm over my eyes because I don't want to see him take the money; I don't want to see him go....

He might say something. He might say good night, or good-bye, or good luck or something.

The door shuts.

When he has gone I turn over on my side and huddle up, making myself as small as possible, my knees almost touching my chin. I cry in the way that hurts right down, that hurts your heart and your stomach. Who is this crying? The same one who laughed on the landing, kissed him and was happy. This is me, this is myself, who is crying. The other – how do I know who the other is? She isn't me.

Her voice in my head: 'Well, well, well, just think of that now. What an amusing ten days! Positively packed with thrills. The last performance of What's-her-name And Her Boys or It Was All Due To An Old Fur Coat. Positively the last performance. ... Go on, cry, allez-y. Encore. Tirez, as they say here. ... Now, calm, calm, say it all out calmly. You've had dinner with a beautiful young man and he kissed you and you've paid a thousand francs for it. Dirt cheap at the price, especially with the exchange the way it is. Don't forget the exchange, dearie – but of course you wouldn't, would you? And you've picked up one or two people in the street and you've bought a picture. Don't forget the picture, to remind you of – what was it to remind you of? Oh, I know – of human misery....'

He'll stare at me, gentle, humble, resigned, mocking, a little mad. Standing in the gutter playing his banjo. And I'll look back at him because I shan't be able to help it, remembering about being young, and about being made love to and making love, about pain and dancing and not being afraid of death, about all the music I've ever loved, and every time I've been happy. I'll look back at him and I'll say: 'I know the words to the tune you're playing. I know the words to every tune you've ever played on your bloody banjo. Well, I mustn't sing any more – there you are. Finie la chanson. The song is ended. Finished.'

Then I shall think of this hotel, the exact shape of the bed and the comic papers in the lavatory. There was that quite ordinary joke that made me laugh so much because it was signed God. Just like that – G-O-D, God. Joke, by God. And what a sense of humour! Even the English aren't in it.

She says: 'I hate to stop you crying. I know it's your favourite pastime, but I must remind you that the man next door has probably heard every damned thing that's happened and is now listening-in to the sequel. Not exactly what one would have expected, perhaps. But still – quite amusing.'

I stop crying. I stretch my legs out. I feel very tired.

'And another thing,' she says. 'If he's taken all the money – which he almost certainly has – that'll be a lovely business, won't it?'

I get up and blow my nose. There is blood on the handkerchief. I look in the glass and see that my mouth is swollen, and it is still bleeding where he bit it. I go over to the dressing-case.

'Go on, look. You might as well know.'

I feel in the right-hand pocket, take the money out and look at it. Two hundred-franc notes, a mille note.

'Well! *What* a compliment! Who'd have thought it?'

'I knew,' I say, 'I knew. That's why I cried.'

I get the tooth-glass and half-fill it with whisky. Here's to you, gigolo, chic gigolo. ... I bow deeply. Have another. ...

I have another.

I appreciate this, sweet gigolo, from the depths of my heart. I'm not used to these courtesies. So here's to you. And here's to you. ...

*

I am very drunk. I see the Russian's face and his mouth moving, saying: 'Madame Vénus se fâchera.' 'Oh, her!' I say. 'What do I care about her? She's never done anything for me except play me a lot of dirty tricks.' 'She does that to everybody,' he says. 'All the same, be careful of her. Take care, take care. ...'

A hum of voices talking, but all you can hear is 'Femmes, femmes, femmes, femmes. ...' And the noise of a train saying: 'Paris, Paris, Paris, Paris. ...' Madame Vénus is angry and Phoebus Apollo is walking away from me down the boulevard to hide himself in la crasse. Only address: Mons P. Apollo, La Crasse. ... But I know quite well that all this is hallucination, imagination. Venus is dead; Apollo is dead; even Jesus is dead.

All that is left in the world is an enormous machine, made of white steel. It has innumerable flexible arms, made of steel. Long, thin arms. At the end of each arm is an eye, the eyelashes stiff with mascara. When I look more closely I see that only some of the arms have these eyes – others have lights. The arms that carry the eyes and the arms that carry the lights are all extraordinarily flexible and very beautiful. But the grey sky, which is the background, terrifies me. ... And the arms wave to an accompaniment of music and of song. Like this: 'Hotcha

– hotcha – hotcha. ...' And I know the music; I can sing the song. ...

I have another drink. Damned voice in my head, I'll stop you talking. ...

I am walking up and down the room. She has gone. I am alone.

It isn't such a long time since he left.

Put your coat on and go after him. It isn't too late, it isn't too late. For the last time, for the last time. ...

Well, I can't, my dear. Not because I'm too proud or anything like that, but because my legs feel funny.

'Come back, come back,' I say. Like that. Over and over again. 'You must come back, you shall come back. I'll force you to come back. No, that's wrong. ... I mean, please come back, I beg you to come back.'

I press my hands over my eyes and I see him. He is walking along the Boulevard St Michel towards Montparnasse, thinking: 'Sale femme. Ridiculous woman.'

'Come back, come back, come back,' I say.

He doesn't hear.

He is walking along as quickly as he can. He is cold and vexed.

'You don't like men, and you don't like women either. You like nothing, nobody. Sauf ton sale cerveau. Alors, je te laisse avec ton sale cerveau. ...'

(A monster. ... The monster that can only crawl, or fly. ... Ah! but fly. ...)

'But why the gesture of not taking the money?' I argue. 'It was simply ridiculous. You know you're regretting it already. Go back and get it. You could walk in, you could say "I forgot something", take it and walk out again.'

Come back, come back, come back. ...

This is the effort, the enormous effort, under which the human brain cracks. But not before the thing is done, not before the mountain moves.

Come back, come back, come back....

He hesitates. He stops. I have him.

'Listen. You hear me now, don't you? It's quite early – not twelve yet. The door will still be open. All you've got to do is to walk upstairs. If anybody speaks to you, say: "The woman in number forty-one, she expects me; she's waiting for me." Say that.'

I see him, very clearly, in my head. I daren't let him go for a moment.

Come back, come back, come back....

He mustn't have to knock, I think. He must be able to walk straight in.

I get up and try to put the key on the outside of the door. I drop it. I leave the door a little open.

'I've got all my clothes on,' I think. 'How stupid!'

I undress very quickly. I am watching every step he takes.

Now he is turning into the end of the street. Very clear he is in my head. He is turning into the end of my street. I see the houses....

I get into bed. I lie there trembling. I am very tired.

Not me, no. Don't worry, it's my sale cerveau that's so tired. Don't worry about that – no more sale cerveau.

I think: 'How awful I must look! I must put the light out.'

But it doesn't matter. Now I am simple and not afraid; now I am myself. He can look at me if he wants to. I'll only say: 'You see, I cried like that because you went away.'

(Or did I cry like that because I'll never sing again, because the light in my sale cerveau has gone out?)

Now he has come up to the hotel.

He presses the button and the door opens.

He is coming up the stairs.

Now the door is moving, the door is opening wide. I put my arm over my eyes.

He comes in. He shuts the door after him.

I lie very still, with my arm over my eyes. As still as if I were dead. . . .

I don't need to look. I know.

I think: 'Is it the blue dressing-gown, or the white one? That's very important. I must find that out – it's very important.'

I take my arm away from my eyes. It is the white dressing-gown.

He stands there, looking down at me. Not sure of himself, his mean eyes flickering.

He doesn't say anything. Thank God, he doesn't say anything. I look straight into his eyes and despise another poor devil of a human being for the last time. For the last time. . . .

Then I put my arms round him and pull him down on to the bed, saying: 'Yes – yes – yes. . . .'

READ MORE IN PENGUIN

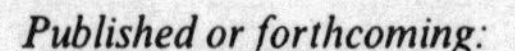
Published or forthcoming:

Ulysses James Joyce

Written over a seven-year period, from 1914 to 1921, *Ulysses* has survived bowdlerization, legal action and bitter controversy. An undisputed modernist classic, its ceaseless verbal inventiveness and astonishingly wide-ranging allusions confirm its standing as an imperishable monument to the human condition. 'Everybody knows now that *Ulysses* is the greatest novel of the century' Anthony Burgess, *Observer*

Nineteen Eighty-Four George Orwell

Hidden away in the Record Department of the Ministry of Truth, Winston Smith skilfully rewrites the past to suit the needs of the Party. Yet he inwardly rebels against the totalitarian world he lives in, which controls him through the all-seeing eye of Big Brother. 'His final masterpiece . . . *Nineteen Eighty-Four* is enthralling' Timothy Garton Ash, *New York Review of Books*

The Day of the Locust *and* The Dream Life of Balso Snell
Nathanael West

These two novellas demonstrate the fragility of the American dream. In *The Day of the Locust*, talented young artist Todd Hackett has been brought to Hollywood to work in a major studio. He discovers a surreal world of tarnished dreams, where violence and hysteria lurk behind the glittering façade. 'The best of the Hollywood novels, a nightmare vision of humanity destroyed by its obsession with film' J. G. Ballard, *Sunday Times*

The Myth of Sisyphus Albert Camus

The Myth of Sisyphus is one of the most profound philosophical statements written this century. It is a discussion of the central idea of absurdity that Camus was to develop in his novel *The Outsider*. Here Camus poses the fundamental question – Is life worth living? – and movingly argues for an acceptance of reality that encompasses revolt, passion and, above all, liberty.

READ MORE IN PENGUIN

Published or forthcoming:

Love in a Cold Climate and Other Novels Nancy Mitford

Nancy Mitford's brilliantly witty, irreverent stories of the upper classes in pre-war London and Paris conjure up a world of glamour and decadence, in which her heroines deal with hilariously eccentric relatives, the excitement of love and passion, and the thrills of the Season. But beneath their glittering surfaces, Nancy Mitford's novels are also hymns to a lost era and to the brevity of life and love.

The Prime of Miss Jean Brodie Muriel Spark

Romantic, heroic, comic and tragic, schoolmistress Jean Brodie has become an iconic figure in post-war fiction. Her glamour, freethinking ideas and manipulative charm hold dangerous sway over her girls at the Marcia Blaine Academy, who are introduced to a privileged world of adult games that they will never forget. 'A sublimely funny book ... unforgettable and universal' Candia McWilliam

Sons and Lovers D. H. Lawrence

Gertrude Morel, a delicate yet determined woman, no longer loves her boorish husband and devotes herself to her sons, William and Paul. Inevitably there is conflict when Paul falls in love and seeks to escape his mother's grasp. Lawrence's modern masterpiece reflects the transition between the past and the future, between one generation and the next, and between childhood and adolescence.

Cold Comfort Farm Stella Gibbons

When the sukebind is in the bud, orphaned, expensively educated Flora Poste descends on her relatives at Cold Comfort Farm. There are plenty of them – Amos, called by God; Seth, smouldering with sex; and, of course, Great Aunt Ada Doom, who saw 'something nasty in the woodshed' ... 'Very probably the funniest book ever written' Julie Burchill, *Sunday Times*

READ MORE IN PENGUIN

Published or forthcoming:

A Confederacy of Dunces John Kennedy Toole

A monument to sloth, rant and contempt, a behemoth of fat, flatulence and furious suspicion of anything modern – this is Ignatius J. Reilly of New Orleans. In magnificent revolt against the twentieth century, he propels his monstrous bulk among the flesh-pots of a fallen city, a noble crusader against a world of dunces. 'A masterwork of comedy' *The New York Times*

Giovanni's Room James Baldwin

Set in the bohemian world of 1950s Paris, *Giovanni's Room* is a landmark in gay writing. David is casually introduced to a barman named Giovanni and stays overnight with him. One night lengthens to more than three months of covert passion in his room. As he waits for his fiancée to arrive from Spain, David idealizes his planned marriage while tragically failing to see Giovanni's real love.

Breakfast at Tiffany's Truman Capote

It's New York in the 1940s, where the Martinis flow from cocktail-hour to breakfast at Tiffany's. And nice girls don't, except, of course, Holly Golightly. Pursued by Mafia gangsters and playboy millionaires, Holly is a fragile eyeful of tawny hair and turned-up nose. She is irrepressibly 'top banana in the shock department', and one of the shining flowers of American fiction.

Delta of Venus Anaïs Nin

In *Delta of Venus* Anaïs Nin conjures up a glittering cascade of sexual encounters. Creating her own 'language of the senses', she explores an area that was previously the domain of male writers and brings to it her own unique perceptions. Her vibrant and impassioned prose evokes the essence of female sexuality in a world where only love has meaning.

BY THE SAME AUTHOR

After Leaving Mr Mackenzie

After being left by Mr Mackenzie (and not the other way around) Julia faces facts. But standing on her own is more difficult than she thought – she is restricted by the very existence she has created. *After Leaving Mr Mackenzie* is a brilliant, yet brutal, portrait of a woman struggling to retrieve both life and love.

'One of the finest British writers this century' A. Alvarez

Voyage in the Dark

'It was as if a curtain had fallen, hiding everything I had ever known', says Anna, 18 years old and catapulted to England from the West Indies after the death of her beloved father. Working as a chorus girl, Anna drifts into the demi-monde of Edwardian London. But there, dismayed by the unfamiliar cold and greyness, she is absolutely alone, and unconsciously floating from innocence to harsh experience.

'A wonderful bitter-sweet book, written with disarming simplicity' Esther Freud, *Express*

Quartet

Set against a background of winter-wet streets and smoke-filled cafés, Jean Rhys's first novel is both poignant and disturbingly intimate in its vivid depiction of a woman on her own.

'She is loved not just for a talent that seems as spontaneous and individual in its personality as physical beauty, but for a special kind of courage' *Guardian*

Wide Sargasso Sea

Inspired by Charlotte Brontë's *Jane Eyre* and drawing upon memories of her own Caribbean childhood, this classic study of betrayal is Jean Rhys's brief, beautiful masterpiece.

'Rhys took one of the works of genius of the 19th century and turned it inside-out to create one of the works of genius of the 20th century' Michèle Roberts, *The Times*